ADVENTURE THRU'
THE BIBLE

Discovering The Hidden Treasures of God's Word

CHRISTIAN EMPHASIS SERIES

ADVENTURE THRU' THE BIBLE

Discovering The Hidden Treasures of God's Word

Deepak Kharel

ISPCK
2006

Adventure Thru' The Bible — Published by the Rev. Dr. Ashish Amos of the Indian Society for Promoting Christian Knowledge (ISPCK), Post Box 1585, 1654 Madarsa Road, Kashmere Gate, Delhi-110006 under the Christian Emphasis Series.

ISBN : 81-7214-933-6

Cover Design: Koshy Prakash

Laser typeset at **ISPCK,** Post Box 1585, 1654, Madarsa Road, Kashmere Gate, Delhi-110006.

Tel: 23866323, Fax: 91-11-23865490

e-mail: ashish@ispck.org.in • mail@ispck.org.in

website: www.ispck.org.in

Dedication

This book entitled "Adventure Thru' The Bible"
is lovingly and prayerfully dedicated to those
men and women of God who really hunger and
thirst for the hidden treasures of God's Word.

And

My beloved wife Mrs. Nirmala and
children Vinita and Aasha.

CONTENTS

Chapter- 3

INTRODUCTION TO THE SERIES

How is the Word of God known here in the twenty first century? Who gets to name God? Can human beings speak for God? How can we distinguish between our wishful thinking about God and legitimate constraints? What will prevent us from confusing God's words of comfort with our own idolatrous longings? Does anybody believe any more that this is remotely possible? Does God still speak?

Christian publishers of the modern age are burdened with such questions in today's fast changing environment with technological advancement, new economic environment, liberalisation and unbridled consumerism. The entire value system faces a big challenge in modern times.

The church is struggling to keep its followers and priorities intact. One often sees that the youth of today are struggling to keep their faith strong. They often get disillusioned as the church does not seem to provide them solutions to face modern day challenges. The ISPCK is faced with this important task of preparing such material for the church and its followers, which will help them to understand their faith better in their own context, strengthening them to retain Christian values amidst such materialism. The Christian Emphasis Series is a result of this, under which this book on "Adventure Thru' The Bible", is published.

Rev. Dr. Ashish Amos
General Secretary
ISPCK

ACKNOWLEDGEMENTS

First and foremost, glory, praise and honour to be the God the Father , the Son and the Holy Spirit who revealed Himself through the Bible and whose unfailing love and care led us thus far.

Secondly, I express heartfelt appreciation to Rev. Dr. John Thannickal, *the Founder and Principal of New Life College* and his family. A special thanks goes to Rev. Ken Henson and his family, and NLC family as a whole.

Thirdly, I would like to give thanks to Bro. Isaac, Bro. Joji, Bro. Josh Thomas, Jeevan Magar and Twang, for helping me in typing the hand written manual of this book. A special remark of thanks goes to Bro. Koshy Prakash for cover designing.

Fourthly, I want to lovingly thank Bro. Bindra Bahadur Rai for helping me in different ways, whose brotherly love and respect was my source of encouragment during the adventure.

Finally, many thanks go to all known and unknown, financial and prayer supporters and well wishers. May the good God, bless and help all of us in the adventure of enjoining in His priceless treasures.

Deepak Kharel
Suryapura – 3,
Rupandehi, Nepal

INTRODUCTION

It is the most important and urgent need that a Bible student (*the one who has the hunger and the thirst for knowing the God's Word*) obtain a fantastic grasp of the Bible as a whole. However, in order to grasp the hidden treasures of the Bible , he or she must first gain an understanding of the little bit of Bible background as well as of each books of it that makes up the book.

This book is designed in such a way that every one finds it very easy to study the Bible in a systematic way. However, we should always understand very clearly that any book , whatever it may be, cannot be a substitute for the Bible, the living Word of God. So, "*Adventure Thru' The Bible*" is just a small book that will help you understand the Bible.

The format of this book is very simple, straight forward and unique. It has mainly three chapters. First chapter deals briefly with understanding the Bible where the meaning of the 'Bible', its origin, cannonization, its message for today, some inspiring comments of the men and women of God concerning Bible, different methods of the Bible study, Bible and Science so on and so forth has been mentioned as the gateway to the adventure through the whole Bible. Second and the third chapters are adventures through the whole Bible, book by book. It is designed to present a systematic glimpse of each book of the Bible i.e., from Genesis through the Revelation. This has been done by applying the following points to each book.

1. An Introduction
This is an introductory part of the book which introduces the book briefly.

2.   Authorship and Date

In this title, the writer of the particular book and the approximate date of writing has been given by the help of different commentaries and the related books.

3.   Purpose of the Book

Under this title, the main purpose of the writer which he/she had in his/her mind while writing the books of the Holy Bible under the guidance and the supervision of the Holy Spirit, has been presented in lucid form.

4.   Theology and Theme

This title gives the main thrust of the book. A little bit of the theological theme has been introduced to motivate the reader to emerge into the deeper dimension of theology. Actually, theology is the study of God. In other words, it is the study of God's dealing with mankind. In a broader sense , theology is *theo-centric* as well as *anthropo-centric*.

5.   Christology

Christology is the study of the Person and the Work of Christ. In this section, an attempt has been made to explore the Person and the Work of Christ in each book of the Bible.

6.   Pneumatology

It is the study of the Person and the Work of the Holy Spirit. Here, it has been presented how the Holy Spirit is on the move in each book of the Bible. In other words, the function and the role of the Holy Spirit in each book of the Holy Bible is given in a nutshell.

7.   Outline

In this section, an outline of the book has been given. This will help the student of the Bible to study it in systematic way. This outline has been prepared according to the topic, title and the related subjects.

8. Application

The Bible is the Word of God. It is the inspired Word of God given to all human being of all the ages through the chosen men and women of God by the empowerment of the Holy Spirit. It is the timeless book with the life changing and life challenging application at all the times. In this section, the application of the each book of the Bible has been given.

CHAPTER – 1

UNDERSTANDING THE BIBLE

THE MEANING OF THE BIBLE

The word "Bible" is of Greek origin and simply means – the book or the books. In the sense which it now has throughout the world, it was first used in the fourth century by the Greek father, Chrysostom, but it was so natural to the Christian to designate the volume which contains the standard of their faith and duty and the foundation of their hope as -the Book, that the word was transferred from Greek into Latin and thence into all modern languages. Eventually, the plural form *biblia* was used by Latin speaking Christians to denote all the books of the Old Testament and the New Testaments. Before that time, the Christians generally designated the collection of their religious books by terms corresponding to our scriptures, holy writings, sacred writings etc. The name Bible commonly used to designate the thirty-nine books of the Old Testament and twenty seven books of the New Testament. These sixty six books constitute a divine library that is nevertheless, in a vital sense, one Book.

The Bible is the book of books – God's written revelation of His will to mankind. The Bible not only contains the Word of God, it is the Word of God, specially and supernaturally given by God to man by Divine inspiration[1] (II Tim. 3:16). God caused the writers to write exactly what He wanted. The Bible contains the plan of

---

[1] The real meaning of the word is that God breathed out scripture. In both Hebrew and Greek words for breath and Spirit are the same. The word inspiration shows that the Spirit's work included the inspiration of scripture. The doctrine of inspiration doesn't mean that God dictated the words for the people to write. Rather, as each man wrote according to his God-given character, insight and purpose, God was breathing through him to ensure that these human words were also the unchangeable Word of God.

God for every person in the world. There are two testaments in the Bible. The word 'testament' means covenant or agreement.

1)   The Old Testament contains 39 books.

2)   The New Testament contains 27 books.

The Old Testament is the covenant or agreement God made with man about his salvation before Christ came. The New Testament is the covenant or agreement God made with man about his salvation after Christ came. The Old Testament looks forward to the cross and the New Testament looks back to the cross.

God Himself in a very real sense wrote these books of the Bible. Humanly speaking, 40 men wrote them over a period of about 1600 years. This is the *doctrine of dual authorship*. God inspired men to write exactly what He wanted them to, without forcing them into a mould or distorting their own personalities or abilities to write. These men were kings and princes, poets and philosophers, prophets and statesman, farmers and fishermen.

DIVINE ORIGIN OF THE BIBLE

There are many evidences that the Bible is an entirely unique book, quite unlike any other work. The unique claims within the Bible itself bear witness to its unusual character, some thirty-eight hundred times the Bible declares '*God said*', '*thus says the Lord*'. The testimony of reliable witnesses-particularly by Jesus, but also of others such as Moses, Joshua David, Daniel, Nehemiah in Old Testament and John and Paul in the New Testament – affirmed the authority and verbal inspiration of the Holy Scripture.

The Bible stands distinct from other religious writings. For example, the Islamic Koran was compiled by an individual, Zaid Ibn Thabit, under the guidance of Mohammed's father-in-law, Abu-Bakr. Additionally, in A.D 650, a group of Arab scholars produced a unified version and destroyed all the previous copies to preserve the unity of the Koran. By contrast, the Bible comes from some 40 different authors from diverse vocations in life. For instance, among the writers of scriptures were Moses, a political leader; Joshua, a military leader; David, a shepherd; Solomon, a king; Amos, a herdsman and fruit pincher; Daniel, a prime-minister; Matthew, a tax collector; Luke, a medical doctor; Paul, a rabbi; and Peter, a fisherman.

Moreover, the Bible was not only written by a diversity of authors, but also in different locations and under a variety of circumstances. In fact, it was written in three continents, Europe Asia and Africa. Paul wrote from the Roman prison as well as from the city of Corinth – both in Europe; Jeremiah (perhaps Moses) wrote from Egypt in Africa; most of the other books were written in Asia. Moses probably wrote in the desert, David composed his Psalms in the country side, Solomon contemplated the Proverbs in the royal courts, John wrote as a banished person on the island of Patmos and Paul wrote 5 books from prison.

It is apparent that many of the writers did not know of the other writers of scripture and were unfamiliar with the other writings, in as much as the writers wrote over a period of more than 1600 years, yet the Bible is a marvelous, unified whole. That is to say that there are no contradictions or inconsistencies within its pages. The Holy Spirit is the unifier of the 66 books, determining its harmonious consistency. In unity, these books teach the Trinity of God, the deity of Jesus Christ, the personality of the Holy Spirit, the fall and depravity of man, as well as salvation by grace.[2]

DIVINE REVELATION OF THE BIBLE

The word "revelation" means 'disclosure' or 'unveiling', hence, revelation signifies God unveiling Himself to mankind. Rom. 16:25, Luke 2:32 indicates that God has unveiled Himself in the Person of Jesus Christ. That is the epitome of God's revelation. Revelation is a act of God, whereby He discloses Himself or communicates truth to the mankind, whereby He makes manifest to His creatures that which could not be known in any other way. Revelation

---

[2] True religion is not a matter of obeying rules or having mystical experiences but of experiencing God's grace. Grace is the manifestation of God's love and mercy towards sinful humanity (II Cor. 8:9, I Timothy 2:11). It is an unmerited favour of God towards us. Divine grace provides not only salvation but security also.

signifies God's disclosure of Himself through creation, history, the conscience of man and scripture. It is given in both events and word. There are two kinds of revelations: general revelation and the special revelation of which a brief description is given below:

General Revelation

General revelation is God revealing certain truths and aspects about His nature to all humanity, which revelation is essential and preliminary to God's special revelation. God's revelation in nature is perhaps the most prominent demonstration of general revelation (Psalm 19:1-6). No one is excluded from this revelation of God. Whenever man peers at the universe, there is orderliness. At a distance of 93 million miles from the earth, the sun provides exactly the right temperature environment for man to function on earth. The entire human body - its cardio- vascular system, the bone structure, the respiratory system, the muscles, the nervous system including its center in the brain - reveals an infinite God. God has revealed Himself through conscience (Rom. 2:14-15). Man initiatively knows not only that God's values goodness and abhors evil but also that He is ultimately accountable to such righteous power. Conscience may be regarded as an inner monitor or the voice of God in the soul, that passes judgment on man's response to the moral law within.

Special Revelation

Special revelation involves a narrower focus than general revelation and is restricted to Jesus Christ and the scripture. Special revelation has been necessitated because of man's sinful estate through the fall. In order to restore fallen humanity to fellowship with Himself, it was essential that God revealed the way of salvation and reconciliation[3] hence, the essence of special revelation centres on the Person of Jesus Christ. He is displayed in scripture as the one who has explained the Father (John 1:18). There was human authorship of the scripture but the Holy Spirit superintended the

---

[3] Reconciliation means a change from being enemies to being friend. It is the change which Christ's death produced in the relationship between God

writers (II Pet. 1:21), ensuring an inerrant Word. The Bible accurately presents the special revelation of God in Christ.

CANONIZATION OF THE SCRIPTURE (BIBLE)

Those books, which were recognized as divinely inspired, were placed in the canon. 'Canon' means the collection of approved books which came up to the standard and therefore served as the testing rule for faith and practice.

Protestant Canon: There are 39 in the Old Testament and 27 in the New Testament in the Protestant canonization of the scripture. They are:

Old Testament

1. *Pentateuch:* Genesis, Exodus, Leviticus, Numbers, Deuteronomy.

2. *Historical Books:* Joshua, Judges, Ruth, I Samuel, II Samuel, I Kings, II Kings, I Chronicles, II Chronicles, Ezra, Nehemiah, Esther.

3. *Poetical Books:* Job, Psalms, Proverbs, Ecclesiastes, Song of Solomon.

4. *Major Prophets:* Isaiah, Jeremiah, Lamentation, Ezekiel, Daniel.

5. *Minor Prophets:* Hosea, Joel, Amos, Obadiah, Jonah, Micah, Nahum, Habakkuk, Zephaniah, Haggai, Zechriah, Malachi.

New Testament

1. *Gospels and History:* Matthew, Mark, Luke, John, Acts.

2. *Letters:*

   Doctrinal: Romans, Galatians, I Corinthians, II Corinthians

   Prison Epistles: Ephesians, Philippians, Colossians, Philemon.

   Pastoral Epistles: I Timothy, II Timothy, Titus.

   Johannine Epistles: I John, II John, III John.

   Petruine Epistles: I Peter, II Peter

---

and man. Christians can participate in the ministry of reconciliation by imploring sinners to be 'reconciled to God' (II Cor. 5:19,20).

General Epistles: I Thessalonians, II Thessalonians, Hebrews, James, Jude.

3.   *Prophecy*: Revelation.

FACTORS CONSIDERED IN THE PROCESS OF CANONIZATION

There were basically five guidance factors used to determine whether or not a book is cononical or scripture. Following are the basic principles used for canonization.

1.   *Is it authoritative*? Here they tested whether the books did come from God and they looked for divine authority and source like, "thus says the Lord".

2.   *Is it prophetic*? Here they checked whether the books were written by a man of God?

3.   *Is it authentic*? Here they tested whether the books were written by the author himself or by some one else?

4.   *Is it dynamic*? Here they tested whether the books had life transforming power of God?

5.   *Was it received, collected, read and used by other authors of the Bible.*

     E.g.: Daniel received and read the book of Jeremiah (Daniel 9:2), Peter acknowledged Paul's writings as scripture (II Pet. 3: 14-16) Mark wrote under Peter's authority and Luke wrote under Paul's authority.

6.   *The books should bear evidence* of high moral and spiritual values that would reflect a work of the Holy Spirit.

INSPIRING COMMENTS ON THE BIBLE

There are many men and women of God who have given their comments on the Bible. Some of them are as follows:

*   "The Bible is the only book by which you may know certainly the future; it in the only book that satisfactorily answers the fundamental questions, where did I come from ? Why am I here? Where am I going?" - *Anonymous*

* "The Bible is a window in this prison world, through which we may look into eternity." - *Timothy Dwight*

* "The Bible grows more beautiful, as we grow in our understanding of it."- *Johan W. Von Goethe*

* "It is impossible to mentally or socially enslave a Bible reading people." - *Horace Greeley*

* "Holy Scripture is a stream of running water. Where alike the elephant may swim and the lamb walk without loosing its feet." - *Pope Gregory, the great*

* "The Bible is the greatest benefit which the human race has ever experienced." - *Immanuel Kant*

* "Sin will keep you from Bible. Bible will keep you from sin." - *D.L. Moody*

* "I know that the Bible is inspired because it inspires me." - *D.L. Moody*

* "The Bible is the telescope between man and God." - *A.H. Strong*

* "The Bible is the book of faith and a book of doctrine and a book of morals and a book of religion, of special revelation from God." - *Danie Webster*

* "While some books inform and others reform, only the Bible transforms." - *Billy Graham*

* "The Bible of man's complete ruin in sin and God's complete remedy in Christ." - *C.H. Spurgeon*

* Only the Bible has the answer to the problems of today's world. - *John Haggai*

Hereby I would like to quote a beautiful poem on the Bible that will give us the panorama of the Living Word Of God:

> *Here is the spring where waters flow,*
> *To quench our heart of sin,*
> *Here is the tree where truth doth grow,*
> *To lead our lives therein :*

Here is the judge that slints the strife,
  When men's devices fail:
Here is the bread that feeds the life,
  That death cannot assail.
The tidings of salvation dear,
  Comes to our ears from hence:
The fortress of our faith is here,
  And shield of our defense.
Then be not like the swine that hath,
  A pearl at his desire,
And takes more pleasure from the through
And wallowing in the mire.
Read not this book in any case, but with a single eye:
  Read not first desire God's grace, to understand thereby.
Pray still in faith in this respect, to bear good fruit therein,
  That knowledge may bring this effect, to mortify our sin.
Then happy you shall be in all your life,
  What so to you befalls:
Yes, double happy you shall be
When God by death you calls.

(From the first Bible printed in Scotland)

THE BIBLE: WORD OF GOD FOR TODAY

The Bible is a historical document, inspired infallible and inerrant, sharper than any two edged sword and essential for teaching, rebuking, correcting and training in righteousness (II Tim. 3:16, Heb. 4:12, II Pet. 1:21). The Bible offers the message of abundant life and eternal hope to those who are eternally lost and alienated from God.

When the biblical gospel is brought to people of another culture, change takes place in at least three ways:

1) The Bible as the prophetic Word of God judges and destroys all forms of idolatry in the receptor culture, since idolatry is the way sin against God is expressed in religious categories.

2) The biblical gospel redeems and transforms those elements of culture that do not conflict with God's general revelation

(evaluating all cultures according to its own criteria of truth and righteousness).

3) When the biblical gospel breaks in upon another culture, it brings with its new dimensions of truth which are unique to the gospel. This uniqueness is seen primarily in Jesus Christ whose incarnation[4] gave new meaning to live and to servanthood, whose death on the cross opens up new depths of understanding of forgiveness and divine grace and of suffering and whose resurrection and promised return gives a totally new content to the concept of hope.

THE MESSAGE OF THE BIBLE

The message of the Bible is God's story given through the history of a particular people, whereby He confronts us with Himself and His will for our lives. It centres around what He has done, is doing and will do for us and for our salvation through Jesus Christ.

The Bible's central message is the story of salvation, and throughout both Testaments, three strands in this unfolding story can be distinguished: the harbinger of salvation, the way of salvation and the heirs of salvation. This could be rewarded in terms of the covenant idea by saying that the central message of the Bible is God's covenant with men, and that the strands are the mediator of the covenant, the basis of the covenant and the covenant people. God Himself is the saviour of His people. It is He who confirms His covenant mercy with them. The harbinger of salvation, the mediator of the covenant, is Jesus Christ, the Son of God. The way of salvation, the basis of the covenant, is God's grace, calling forth from His people a response of faith and obedience. The heir of salvation, the covenant people, are the Israel of God, the church of God.

The message of the Bible is God's message to man, communicated in many and various ways (Heb. 1:1) and finally

---

[4] (Lat. = becoming flesh). It is the process whereby Christ the Word, who was with God and was God (John 1:1), became man (John 1: 14). The second Person of the triune Godhead became a thenthropic Person, lived a sinless life in a real human body on earth and died a vicarious death to provide salvation and security for fallen humanity.

incarnated in Christ. Thus the authority of the Holy Scripture, for which it ought to be believed and obeyed, dependeth not upon the testimony of any man or church, but wholly upon the God (who is Truth itself), the author thereof; and therefore it is to be received, because it is the Word of God.

HOW TO STUDY THE BIBLE MEANINGFULLY

1.   The Bible must be studied as a book about God, particularly about God made known in Jesus Christ, in His living relationship with men. Unless God is the first concern of our life or unless we are willing to have Him become so, we shall never understand the Bible. For all the Bible writers, God was the one centre fact of life, from which all the other facts take their meaning. The Bible claims gospel, 'good news' about God in Christ. To understand it, it must be read in that light.

2.   If the living God really speaks in the Bible, it should be studied as God's Word to us in our lives now. The God who spoke long ago, speaks today. Hence, the Bible is not to be read merely as a record of God's dealings with His ancient people. It is the instrument through which God speaks personally to us, its study is incomplete. To read the Bible rightly, is to listen for God's voice to us now in the situation we face.

3.   The Bible must be studied in faith. It is the record of God's action in history which led men to believe in Him (John 20:31). The Bible is designed to persuade, to lead to decision, to evoke man's yes to what God has done for him in Christ. It cannot, therefore, be rightly read in detachment. If it is to be understood, it requires personal involvement with the God whom it speaks. None outside the faith can ever really be gripped by the meaning of the Bible. It can only speak in power when it ceases to be a record of mere past events and becomes the living story out of which my faith springs. It is only as the Bible is read as the sacred writings which are able to instruct... for salvation that its living truth can be grasped (II Tim. 3:15).

But Christian faith is the gift of God (Eph. 2:8). To read the Bible in faith, then, is not merely a human achievement. It is completely dependent on the gracious action of God's Spirit. The Holy Spirit who brought order out of chaos at the creation (Gen. 1:2), who quickened and directed the response of faith in God's people through all the events recorded in the Bible (Isa. 63:11, 14) and who superintended the process by which the scripture came into being (II Tim. 3:16), is the one who must quicken the response of faith in us and guide us in to all the truth (John 16:13).

"The inseparable companion of Holy Scripture is the Holy Spirit." – Martin Luther

"The Bible cannot be known without faith because it is the Word of God." – John Calvin

To understand the Bible, therefore, it must be read with the heart open to the Spirit of God, to receive from Him the gift of the faith, which quicken our response to this record born of faith.

4. The Bible must be studied in prayer. Prayer is the opening of the life to the Spirit of God, so that He may give us the gift of faith. Ask and it shall be given unto you (Luke 11:9) is a law applicable to the Bible study. The Bible is the medium of God's self-disclosure to men who by their own searching cannot find Him and God does not give Himself to the inattentive, the disinterested, the calloused and dissolute. He offers Himself to those who actively seek Him. Prayer is the active waiting, which is necessary to receiving. The study of the Bible, therefore, should be accompanied by a constant out going of the soul towards God, reverently seeking and joyfully expecting Him to speak to us through His Word. Worthy Bible study is always permeated by the prayer of the Psalmist, *open my eyes, that I may behold the wondrous thing out of thy law* (Psalm 119:18).

5. The Bible must be studied in obedience. Obedience to God's Word enables us to hear Him more clearly. Disobedience silences His voice. Light obeyed brings more light. Light rejected brings night. Valid study of the Bible is the kind of listening for the voice of God which shall quicken love to him to neighbour. And unless that is the mood in which we come to it, our study will be in vain.

A constant familarity with the Bible, bathed in prayer and rooted in obedience, is the best means whereby God may speak His Word of direction in any specific moment of decision.

METHODS OF THE BIBLE STUDY

There are different methods of the Bible study, few methods are briefly explained in the following pages that will be very helpful tools for the lovers of the Word of God.

1. *The Telescopic Method*

Telescope is an optical instrument for magnifying distant objects. The telescopic method of the Bible study is the method where we try to see the hidden treasures of the God's Word by chapter outline and the circumstances of the biblical writer and times. In other words, it is the Bible study by taking a ground sweep of a book or the chapter or trying to find out the main outline and knowing the circumstances under which these were preached.

2. *The Microscopic Method*

Microscope is an instrument for magnifying minute objects. This microscopic method of the Bible study tries to look at the biblical treasures by means of careful and minute observation of the verse or section. It is the minute analysis method. In other words, it is the Bible study by taking a verse or section and analysing it from different point of views.

3. *Topical Method*

This is the study of subjects or topics by the light of the Spirit of God. Jesus studied and taught from the scriptures in that way (Luke 24:27). So did Paul (Acts 17:2, 3). Take some great topic and go through the Bible from Genesis to Revelation, searching for all that the Bible has to say on that topic.

4. *Word Study Method*

This method is the study of the words and the expressions of the Word of God. In this method, a particular word is selected and its original meaning, its significance and different translations are learned from the biblical world of then and now.

5. Biographical Method

It is the study of a particular character of the Bible. In this method, a particular character is taken and is followed from the cradle to the grave.

Howard F. Vos gives some of the methods for the Bible study. Some of them are given below as the examples that will, I believe, aid to the study of the Bible effectively and meaningfully.

A. The Inductive Method

This method emphasizes on the process of reasoning or drawing conclusions from the particular cases. It involves inquiry, investigation, scrutiny and a great deal of stress on observation. It is book method. It is drawing conclusions or generalizations from the particular.

B. The Synthetic Method

There are three different readings in this method.

First reading : – The main theme

Second reading : – Further development of the theme.

Third reading : – The outline of the particular passage or book.

C. The Analytical Method

Analysis is defined as a separation of anything into constituent parts or elements or an examination of anything in it's separate parts, as for instance, the consideration of the words which composes sentence or the various proposition which enter into an argument. In relation to scripture, analysis is a detailed study of a book in order to ascertain it's message in all it's ramification, as such it is the direct opposite of synthesis, which attempts to look at the book as a whole and to determine it's message in general. In the process of analysing, we need to ask WH questions such as Who? What? When? Where? Why? Whom and How?

D. The Biographical Method

Not only does biblical biography provide profitable spiritual instruction for the believer, but it presents to him with a worth while manner of propagating Christian truth. This method provides the truth by their life conversion, and way of living. In this method:

a. Collect all the material which the Bible contains concerning the one.

b. Carefully, study the ancestry of them.

c. See, what was the greatest crisis in this person's life and how did he react/meet it?

d. About him/her friendship and growth.

e. Facts and short comings.

f. The influence his/her character had on the society.

g. Lessons which can be gained from him/her life.

E. The Historical Method

While using the historical method of Bible study, the following points are to be followed:

a. Setting of a book – its place in the life of the writer or the history of the people.

b. Historical narrative represented in the book.

c. Historical importance of the book.

d. Textual evidence and inference of what life was like at the time and in the area comprehended by the book.

Bad attitude towards Bible Study

1. *Negative:* It is the negative approach towards Bible study. In this approach, one says like this, "I won't be able to understand anything, so why bother studying it" (an easy way to coopt-out)

2. *Lazy:* For the lazy people, Bible study just stands like a lot of work to do. For the lazy, Bible study becomes a burden rather than benefit.

3. *Know-it-all:* In this approach, one does not know that he/she does not know the Bible. He /she says like this, "nothing new here, same old stuff. I've heard all along" (don't kid yourself).

Good attitude towards Bible Study

1. *Positive:* I can learn the plan of God, He has for me in His Word.

2. *Receptive:* I want to know the plan of God, not my way, but His way.

3. *Expectant:* God is really going to teach me right from His Word.

4. *Faithful:* I am going to work on this discipline yourself to study because you see the benefits it can give you.

Four types of Bible Students

1. *Dropout* (the non participant): I don't want to, and you can't make me.

2. *Castor Oil:* Bitter, but good for what ails me.

3. *Shredded Wheat:* Dry, but nourishing.

4. *Peaches and Cream:* Just can't get enough?

BIBLE AND SCIENCE

The Bible is not a textbook of science but it is authoritative when it does make a statement in the realm of natural knowledge (Job 40:1,2). The modern scientific mind which rejects the Bible because of the supernatural events related therein is only blinded by its prejudice and bias which is a product of unbelief.

An amazing amount of scientific information is found in the Bible. Many scientific facts are related there. Hundreds and even thousands of years before men 'discovered' them by natural scientific methods.

1. The earth is not supported

Many ancient people thought that the earth was carried on the back of a giant turtle (Hindus), a mighty man Atlas (Greeks), or a set of posts (Egyptians). However, 3500 years before Columbus discovered the earth is not supported. Job declared, He hangeth the earth upon nothing (Job 26:7).

2.   *The earth is not flat*

Also, people believed that the earth was flat and therefore sailors feared sailing too far out for fear of falling off the edge. He (God) who sitteth upon the circle of the earth (I Sam. 40:22) was written to the Jews. 2000 years before Columbus sailed west to discover the Western Hemisphere interestingly, his navigator was a Jew.

3.   *The heavens are controlled by ordinances*

Thousands of years before Sir Isaac Newton (1642 –1727)[5] wrote his Celestial Mechanics or Principia,[6] the Lord informed Job (38:33) that the entire universe was controlled by set ordinances which cause all stars and planets to move with the most precise clock work, known.

4.   *Other scientific facts stated in scripture*

a)   Water cycle (Eccle. 1:7) – river, sea, air, rain, river.

b)   All matter and energy completed at earth's origin (Gen. 2:1, 2). The first law of thermodynamics[7] is that matter is neither created or destroyed.

c)   The universe is decaying (Ps. 102:26).

---

[5] He was a scientific genius of the highest order. Among his many achievements were the formulation of the law of gravitation (the pulling force of the earth), the discovery of the differential calculus and the first correct analysis of white light.

[6] It is the work by Sir Isaac Newton where he stated, " the most beautiful system of the Sun, planets and comets, could only proceed from the counsel and dominion of an intelligent and powerful Being.

[7] Britannica Encyclopedia defines it as the study of the relationships among heat, work, temperature and energy. The three laws of thermo-dynamics describes that changes take place in the properties and predict the equlibrium state of the system. The first law states that whenever energy is converted from one form to another, the total quantity of energy remains the same. The second law states that, in a closed system, the entropy of the system does not decrease. The third law states that, as a system approaches absolute zero, further extraction of energy becomes more and more difficult, eventually becoming theoretically impossible.

d) Life is in the blood (Lev. 17:11). An unborn baby is sustained by his own blood produced within its own body from nourishment provided by the mother.

e) Ocean currents (Ps. 8:18). The Bible stimulated Mathew Mury to research the salts of the seas and produced his work on oceanography.[8] The heavens declare the glory of God, and the firmament showeth his handy work (Ps. 19:1).

BIBLE STATISTICS

It was not until A. D. 1250 that the Bible was divided into chapters. At that time, Cardinal Hugo incorporated chapter divisions into the Latin Bible. In 1551, Robert Estienne introduced a Greek New Testament with the inclusion of verse divisions because of the inaccuracy of the chapter division of Hugo. The first entire English Bible to have verse divisions was the Geneva Bible in 1960.

Total books: 66

Total chapters: 1189

Total verses: 31175

Total words: 810697

Total letters: 3566480

The longest chapter: Psalm 119

The shortest chapter: Psalm 117

Central verse: Psalm 118 : 8

The longest verse: Esther 8 : 9

The shortest verse: John 11 : 35

Book without the word 'God': Esther

Isaiah 37 is equal to II King 19

---

[8] It is defined as the scientific discipline concerned with all aspects of the world's oceans and seas, including their physical and chemical properties, origin and geology and life forms. Oceonography aids in predicting weather and climate, in exploitation of the earth's resources, and in understanding the effects of pollutants.

CHAPTER – 2

ADVENTURE THRU' THE OLD TESTAMENT

PENTATEUCH

Pentateuch is a name given to the first five books of the Old Testament: Genesis, Exodus, Leviticus, Numbers and Deuteronomy. Pentateuch is a Greek word, which means – five volumes. The Hebrew word for these books is Torah which means- the law or the teaching. These books contain information from the time of creation till the time of Moses' death.

The Pentateuch or the five books of Moses, constitutes the first and the most important division of Old Testament. It holds the pride of place in the Jewish Canon. It is traditionally thought to be the work of Moses, who alone of the biblical heroes spoke with God face to face (Exo. 33:11; Deu. 34:10-12).

A Brief Sketch of the Life of Moses

He is considered as the founder of the Jewish religion. He was the son of a Hebrew slave in Egypt (Exo. 2:1-10). Just after he was born, the Pharaoh ordered that all male Hebrew babies were to be killed. Moses' mother made a waterproof basket, placed her baby son in it and hid it in the rushes near the shore of the Nile river. An Egyptian princess, found the basket and adopted baby Moses. Fortunately, she hired Moses' mother to take care of him. In this way, Moses grew up understanding the beliefs and customs of both the Hebrews and the Egyptians.

When Moses was 40 years old, he fled from Egypt because he had killed an Egyptian while trying to defend an Israelite slave.

Moses lived in the wilderness for another 40 years. Then God spoke to him from a bush that looked like as if it was on fire but it was not burning up (Exo. 3:2-4:7).

God told Moses that he was to lead the Israelites out of their slavery in Egypt to a promised land that God would give them. God defeated the Pharaoh by harting the Red Sea for the Israelites to go through safely, and then close it on the Pharaoh's army that tried to follow them (Exo. 12-14). During their 40 years in the wilderness, God guided the people with a cloud during the day and a pillar of fire during the night. Many times, Moses was discouraged because of the grumbling of the people. God gave various laws to Moses, so through them the people would know how to live.

Before leaving this world, he reminded them of the Ten Commandments and other instruments God had given them. He emphasized that God expected love and obedience from them and not grumbling and complaining. Moses died at the age of 120 and was buried in the land of Moab (Det. 34). Moses is often mentioned in the New Testament as the giver of the law that Christ came to fulfill.

GENESIS

Genesis is the book of beginnings. It records not only the beginning of the heavens and the earth and of plant, animal and human life, but of all human institution and relationships. Typically, it speaks of the new birth, the new creation.

With Genesis also begins that progressive self-revelation of God, which culminates in Christ. The three primary names of deity: *Elohim, Jehovah*[9] and *Adonai*[10] and the five most important of the

---

[9] It is the Hebrew word for Lord. The primary meaning of the name Lord (Jehovah) is 'the self-existent one'. In redemptive relation to man, Jehovah has seven compound names : *Jehovah-jireh-* 'the Lord will provide'; *Jehovah-rapha* 'the Lord that heals' (Exo. 15:26), 'the healer of the body, soul and the spirit'; *Jehovah-nissi* 'the Lord our banner' (Exo. 17:8-15); *Jehovah-shalom* 'the Lord our peace'; *Jehovah-ra.ah* 'the Lord my shepherd' (Ps. 23); *Jehovah-tsidkenu* 'the Lord our righteousness'(Jer. 23:6) and *Jehovah-*

compound names occur in Genesis and that is an ordered progression which could not be changed without confusion.

The problem of sin is that it affects man's condition on the earth, and his relation with God and the divine solution of that problem are here in essence.

Genesis enters into the very structure of the New Testament, in which it is quoted above 60 times in 17 books. In a profound sense, therefore, the roots of all subsequent revelation are planted deep by in Genesis and whoever would truly comprehend that revelation must begin here.

Authorship

No verse in the Pentateuch names Moses directly as the author, but there are internal evidences favoring the Mosaic authorship as well as the statement from the New Testament by Jesus and others which leads to this conclusion (Exo. 17:14; Mt. 19:8; Acts 3:23; Rom. 10:5; Rev. 15:3).

Date

There is no specified evidence for when Genesis was exactly written. We know that God divinely inspired him to write about events that occurred when no one was yet alive. Anyway, the 40 year period of Israel's wanderings in the desert, which lasted from c.1446 to c.1406, would have been the most likely time for Moses to write the bulk of what is today known as the Pentateuch.

Purpose

The main purpose of this book is to tell us about the creation of the cosmos, the creation of man, the beginning of the sin in human race, the provision of God for redemption, the selection of one man through whose descendant salvation would be possible, the person and the nature of God and as well as about divine judgment and human responsibility.

---

shammah 'the Lord is present' (Eze. 48:35) which signifies Jehovah's abiding presence with His people (Exo. 33:14,15; Heb. 13:5).

[10] The primary meaning of the word Adonai is Master.

Theology

Four primary streams of theological doctrines are presented in Genesis:

1. Monotheistic[11] God.

2. The creation of mankind in the image of God.

3. The reality of evil. The nature of evil is human defiance of God and disobedience to His standards of righteousness.

4. God, answer to the reality of evil is redemption. God is the initiator of redemptive action. Harmony of fellowship with God and restoration of reconciled fellowship with God are always based on human response of faith and trust.

Christology

Genesis moves from the general to the specific in its messianic predictions: Christ is the seed of the woman (3:5). Christ is seen also in people and event that serves as types. Adam is a type of Him who was to come (Rom. 5:14). Both entered the world through a specific act of God as sinless men. Adam is the head of the old creation: Christ is the head of the new creation, Abel's blood sacrifice points to Christ. Melchizedek equals to Jesus Christ (Heb. 7: 3). Joseph is also a type of Jesus Christ. Both are objects of special love by their fathers, hated by their brothers, rejected as rulers over their brothers, conspired against and sold for silver, are condemned through innocent and raised from humiliation to glory by the power of God.

Pneumatology

The Spirit of God was hovering over the face of the waters (1:2). Thus we find the Spirit involved in creation. The Holy Spirit also worked in Joseph, a fact obvious to Pharaoh (41:38). The Spirit of

---

[11] Monotheism is belief in a single Supreme Being. This was the original faith of the human race and has been held by a faithful minority through out world history. Monotheism formed the basis of the Mosaic Covenant (Exo. 20 : 1-7). It repudiated all idolatry and all physical representations of Deity.

God supernaturally resolved every challenge of the God's chosen families.

Out Line

1. The beginning of world 1: 1-25

2. The beginning of human race 1:26-2:25

3. The beginning of sin in the world 3:1-7

4. The beginning of promise of redemption 3:8-24

5. The beginning of family life 4:1-15

6. The beginning of civilization 4:16-9:29

7. The beginning of nation of the world 10,11

8. The beginning of Hebrew people 12-50

    (i)   Abraham 12:1-25:18

    (ii)   Isaac 25:19-26:35 (Canaan)

    (iii) Jacob 27:1-37:2 (Egypt)

    (iv) Joseph 37:2b -50:26

Genesis begins with God but ends 'in a coffin'. This book is the history of human failure. But we find that God meets every failure. He is a glorious Savior.

Application

Abraham is our example of faith (15:6 and Gal. 3:7). Joseph's life is an exquisite sermon for all who suffer unfairly and is a challenge to faithfulness in this age of undisciplined permissiveness. When Adam sinned, all of us not only sinned but inherited a resident sin nature. Only a savior can deal effectively with this inherited natural corruption.

EXODUS

Exodus is a Greek word which is composed of two parts, *ex* = out and *hodus* = road. The book of Exodus describes the departure of the nation of Israel from their bondage in the land of Egypt. Centuries before the patriarch, Jacob had brought his extended family to Egypt to avoid starvation (Gen. 46:1-27). Because of a shift in political power, the descendents of Joseph and his brothers fell into slavery but they became quite numerous. The emphasis on family in Genesis has given way to a focus upon the nation of Israel in the book of Exodus. They were slowly shaped into people, who were in a covenant relationship with Jehovah God.

Authorship and Date

Moses again claims the authorship for this book. He wrote down the first hand experience he had with God and with the people of Israel. As far as the date of the book is concerned, we can assume that it was written soon after the completion of the tent of meeting (a portable tabernacle) around 1444 BC.

Purpose

Exodus stands as an eternal testimony to the nature of God (who is He) and the works of God (what He does). We can see God's attributes of holiness, power, justice, truth, mercy and glory in this book. The nature of God and His faithfulness to His promise can also be found.

Theme

God delivers the Israelites from the bondage in Egypt, makes them His own treasured possession (19:5). The main theme of Exodus is redemption.[12] All people may have hope, no matter how desperate the situation. God will send a deliverer to display His awesome power and deliverance will come through blood. God keeps His promises. He is faithful.

---

[12] Though closely allied to salvation, redemption is more specific, for it denotes the means by which salvation is achieved, namely, by the payment of a ransom. Redemption is the deliverance through payment of a price or ransom. Exodus is the book of redemption and teaches that : the redemption is wholly of God (Exo. 3:7,8; John 3:16) ; it is through a person (Exo. 2:2; John 3:16, 17) ; it is by blood (Exo. 12:13, 23, 27; I Pet. 1:18) and it is by power (Exo. 6:6, 13:14; Rom. 8:2)

The blood of Christ redeems the believers from the guilt and the penalty of sin (I Pet. 1:18) as the power of the Spirit delivers from the dominion of sin (Rom. 8:2; Eph. 2:2).

Theology

God is the unseen controller of all history and all circumstances (Exo. 1). He over rules all events for the ultimate good of His children, whatever the immediate effects. God is Holy. He desires holiness from us (Lev. 19:2). Unlike the gods of Canaan (I Kings 18:2), God is a living God (Deut. 5:26), a God who acts. Above all, He is the God who acts in salvation (Exo. 3:8).

Pharaoh stands for the height of human power, ranged against God and the people of God: therefore his fall is a fitting symbol, for all time, of the impossibility of striving against God or of thwarting His plans. That is why the crossing of the sea became such a fitting symbol of God's act of salvation.

Christology

Moses is a type of Christ. Both are endangered in infancy, renounced power and wealth deliverers, lawgivers and mediators. Jesus is our Passover Lamb (I Corinth. 5:7). Seven feasts portray the ministry of Jesus. Baptism is considered as Exodus event (Rom. 6:2, 3; I Cor. 10:1, 2). Manna and water equal to Christ (John 6:31-35; I Cor. 10:3, 4). The tabernacle clearly speaks of the Person of Christ and the way of redemption. It is the theology in the physical form. In several ways, the high priest foreshadows the ministry of Christ, our great High Priest (Heb. 4:14-16, 9:11,12, 24-28).

Pneumatology

Oil in the book of Exodus symbolically represents the Holy Spirit (27:20). For example, the anointing oil is a type of the Holy Spirit, which is used to prepare worshippers and priests for godly service (30:31). The fruits of the Holy Spirit are listed in Gal 5:22, 23. A parallel list can also be found in Exo. 34:6,7, which lists the attributes of God as being merciful, gracious, long – suffering good, truthful and forgiving. The most direct references to the Holy Spirit can be found in 31:3-11 and 35:30-36:1 when individuals are empowered by the Holy Spirit to became great artisans. Through the enabling work of the Holy Spirit, these individuals' natural abilities were enhanced and expanded to perform the tasks with excellence and perfections.

D.L. Moody says:

Moses is the great hero who spent

- 40 years thinking he was somebody

- 40 years learning he was nobody

- 40 years discovering what God can do with a nobody (Heb.11:23-29).

Out Line

1. Deliverance 1:1-18:27

   (i) Bondage and oppression 1:1-11:10

   (ii) Deliverance and provision 12:1-18:27

2. Worship 19:1-40:38

   (i) Law 19:1-24:18

   (ii) Tabernacle blueprint 25:1-31:18

   (iii) Idolatry 32:1-34:28

   (iv) Tabernacle construction 35:1-40:38

Application

God blesses those who remain in a covenant relationship with Him. He is their God and they become His holy people. God delivers those who find themselves in bondage. The deliverance may not come immediately, but it will come to those who wait and make preparation for His deliverance. That deliverance is based upon obedience to God's expressed will and upon moving when He says to move.

Tabernacle

Tabernacle was known by several names; dwelling, tent, house of sanctity, temple. The tabernacle symbolism found its fulfillment in Christ. He was tabernacle, priest, alter and sacrifice. He is our High Priest who has passed into heavens now to appear for us and to give us success to the holiest by His blood, the blood of everlasting covenant. God who tabernacled with Israel and with man in the word incarnate (Jn. 1:14), does so still in the Body of Christ (Eph. 2:21) and in the believer (I Cor. 6:19).

Exodus is the historical picture of divine grace in the redemption of humanity by God to Himself by Jesus Christ, who is at once our great apostle (Moses) high priest (Aaron) (Heb. 3:1).

LEVITICUS

The book of Moses is called by the title of 'Leviticus' because it records the duties of the Levites. This book describes the role of sacrifice in God's plan. God gave the content of this book to Moses on Mount Sinai. Much more than a religious book, Leviticus contains regulation for the social life as well as the spiritual life of Israel.

Authorship and Date

Moses wrote the book of Leviticus sometimes before the 'wilderness wandering', it is recorded in the book of Numbers, probably around 1440 BC.

Purpose

Leviticus is God's manual for His people explaining how a sinful man can and must approach holy God and live, lives pleasing in His sight. The main purpose of this book is to show that God is holy and that man is sinful. However, if man recognizes this fact and obeys, he is permitted to approach God.

Theme

The inescapable theme of Leviticus is holiness: God is holy; therefore, the people must approach Him and serve Him in holiness.

Christology

The book of Leviticus is replete with the persons and work of Jesus Christ. Burnt offering = Christ's total offering in submission to His father's will. The meal offering = His sinless service. The peace offering = fellowship with God through Christ. The sin offering =

Christ as our guilt bearer. The trespass offering = Christ's payment. High Priest. Passover = death of the Lamb of God. Christ died on the day of Passover. Unleavened berad = the holy walk of the believers (I Cor. 5:6-8). First fruit = Christ's resurrection as the first fruit of the resurrection of all believers (I Cor. 15 :20 –23). Christ rose on the day of the first fruit.

Pneumatology

Though the term 'Holy Spirit' is never mentioned in the book of Leviticus, God's presence is felt throughout the book. The holiness of God's character is constantly referred to the designation of holiness of the people's actions and worship.

Out Line

1. The way of God 1:1-17:16

    (i) Laws of offering 1:1-7:36
    (ii) Laws of consecration of priest 8:1-19:20
    (iii) Laws of purity 11:1-15:33

2. The walk with God 18:1-27:34

    (i) Holy people 18:1-20:27
    (ii) Holy priests 21:1-22:33
    (iii) Holy times 23:1-25:55
    (iv) Just recompense 26:1-46
    (v) Holy vows 27:1-34

Application

The book of Leviticus has a powerful contemporary and personal application for the life of the church today. The sanctity of God and His great desire for fellowship with His people are clearly seen in the description of the sacrificial system. Holiness, being set apart for a saintly life in fellowship with God, is the primary issue for the people of ancient Israel, as it is for the people of God today.

NUMBERS

Genesis is the book of beginnings, Exodus, the book of redemption and Leviticus, the book of atonement and worship. Numbers on the other hand, is the book of testing. Numbers (*arithmoi*) is so named because the Israelites were twice numbered (Ch 1 and 26), the first time at the beginning of their journey, the second time at the close of the 38 years of wandering in the desert. Numbers is a wilderness book covering the time span from the second month of the second year after the Exodus from Egypt to the tenth month of the 40ᵗʰ year.

Authorship and Date

Moses wrote Numbers towards the end of his life (early 1400 B.C.). He was probably camped with the people of Israel at Moab when he composed it.

Purpose

Numbers is the official record of the Israelites journey from Sinai to Moab. From its pages, we learn of the cause and the cure for the 40 years of wandering in the wilderness. It stands as one of the clearest and dearest illustration of the faithfulness of God's people and His promises.

Theme

Forty years of desert wanderings are God's judgment of disobedient and murmuring Jews, the original generation that fled from Egypt. Now with God's help a new generation of believers is ready to cross the Jordan into the promised rest-land of Canaan.

Christology

Perhaps, the clearest portrait of Christ in Numbers is the bronze serpent on the stake, a picture of the crucifixion (21:4-9), John 3:14. The rock that quenches the thirst of the multitude is also a type of Christ (I Cor. 10:4). Manna is equal to bread of life (John 6:31-33). The pillar of cloud and fire signifies the guidance and presence of Christ. Moreover, Balaam foresees the rulership of Christ (24: 17). The sinners refuse in Christ may be seen in the six cities of refuse. The red heifer sacrifice (Num. 19) is also considered a type of Christ.

Pnuematology

The Holy Spirit is spoken of directly in chapter 11. There the Spirit is depicted as performing two functions: anointing for leadership and inspiring prophecy. Moses expresses the longing that all God's people (not only the few selected leaders) would also receive Holy Spirit and prophecy. This hope of Moses is picked up in Joel 2:28-32 and is ultimately fulfilled in the day of Pentecost (Acts 2:16-21) when the Spirit was poured out and made available to all.

Out Line

1. Preparation for the journey (at Sinai) 1:1-10:10
    Inventory and assignments 1:1-4:49
    Final instruction 5:1-10:10

2. The journey (to Moab) 10:11-21:35
    Sinai to Paran 10:11-12:16
    The spies' report 13:1-33
    The people's complaint 14:1-25
    God's judgment 14:26-45
    Desert wanderings 15:1-17:13
    Kadesh to Moab 18:1-21:35

3. At the gate to the land (at Moab) 22:1-36:13
    New problems 22:1-24:25
    Final preparations 25:1-30:16
    Concluding tasks 31:1-36:13

Application

When God gives a promise, we need to respond with optimism, not pessimism. We need to maintain an attitude of thankfulness to God without grumbling, even when we have great needs (Phil. 4:19). Though God is loving and merciful, He is also just. When mankind repeatedly rejects Him, He must issue judgment (Heb. 9:27); when His children repeatedly disobey, He must chastise, sometimes severely (Heb. 12:3-11).

DEUTERONOMY

Deuteronomy can be approached in different angles: It is the book of the law, it is a series of addresses given by Moses, it is a covenant treaty between the sovereign Lord and His people; it is a compendium of directives that the Lord gives through Moses. It is primarily a covenant renewal document.

Authorship and Date

Deuteronomy is Moses' last message to Israel around 1405 BC., written in the desert, east of the Jordan river (1:1).

Purpose

The book of Deuteronomy is one long plea for sincere obedience to God and His commands.

Theme

If you want to enter, claim and keep Canaan's 'rest land', remember your past (4:32), consider your present (5:33) and look at your future (28:2), through the eyes of obedience.

Deuteronomy reveals a lofty monotheism. It projects that love is a central element of God's nature. This book links ethical conduct with covenant life. It demonstrates the spirit of reformation. It acknowledges the Lord as the unique God of Israel, affirms His love and insists that an appropriate response to the Lord is one of loving obedience. The people of God are Holy people and are to manifest quality of relationship by the way they live in all their relationships.

Christology

The most obvious portraits of Christ is seen in 18:15. Moses is the type of Christ. He fulfills the three offices of prophet (34:10-12), priest (Exo. 32: 31-35) and king (although he was not king, he functioned as the ruler of Israel, 33:4,5).

Pneumatology

The unifying theme throughout the Bible is the redemptive activity of God. Deuteronomy reminds the people that the Spirit of God had been with them from the time of their deliverance from Egypt to the present and that He would continue to guide and protect them if only they would be obedient to the regulations of the covenant.

Out Line

1. Introduction 1:1-5
2. Remembrance of the past 1:6-4:43
3. Commandments for the present 4:44-26:19
4. Options affecting the future 27:1-30:20
5. A change in leadership 31:1-34:12

Deuteronomy, Moses' Upper Desert Discourse, consists of a series of farewell messages by Israel's 120 years old leader. It is addressed to the new generation destined to possess the land of promise to those who survived the wilderness wandering for 40 years. Deuteronomy has also been called the 'Book of Remembrance'.

Application

Our choice determines our destiny (30:19). This book teaches that the relation of God with His people is far more than law. Our love, affection and devotion to the Lord must be the true foundation of all our actions. Loyalty to God is the essence of true piety and holiness. Success, victory, prosperity and happiness all depend upon our obedience to the Father.

HISTORICAL BOOKS

The books from Joshua to Esther are known as the historical books. They give a glimpse of the Old Testament events and happenings in the particular period of time in the past.

JOSHUA

The book of Joshua describes the conquest of the land of Canaan under the leadership of Joshua, the successor of Moses. Joshua was a great man of tremendous faith, courage and leadership ability, who believed that God could do what He promised. The Greek form of the name is 'Jesus' Heb 4:6 (KJV). The deliverance that began with the book of Exodus was completed in the book of Joshua. The book of Joshua is the *'Book of Conquest'*.

Authorship and Date

This book is named after its author, Joshua; the loyal and Godly associate of Moses. Joshua son of Nun, was born in Egypt of the tribe of Ephraim. This book was most likely composed soon after the conquest of Canaan, around 1400 BC.

Purpose

The main purpose was to show how God kept His original promise to Abraham and how the wicked were expelled. Moreover, the purpose of the book of Joshua in the broader sense, is to reveal God's might, justice, mercy and willingness to reward those who fear and obey Him. Also, to document God's working through the servant Joshua.

Theme

God is faithful to His promises. The land of Canaan, promised by God, was waiting to be occupied. Israel would have to fight to obtain what was promised. The obstacles they faced were a part of God's plan to oust the idolatrous and corrupt nations from the land. Victory is secure if obedience is unconditional. Loyalty to God brings victory and prosperity. Disloyalty to God brings failure and destruction.

This book reminds us that God is holy and jealous. He tolerates the worship of no other gods. This God who acts in history (24:2-13) had called Israel into being a nation. He had guided her at every step of her journey. The promised land was to be occupied not by their weapons but by the might of the Lord (24:12).

Christology

Joshua himself was the type of Christ. Joshua in Hebrew means Yahweh is salvation and in Greek 'Jesus'. Joshua led the people of God into the possession of their promised inheritance, just as Christ leads us into possession of eternal life.

The scarlet cord in Rahab's window (2:18,21) illustrates Christ's redemptive work on the cross. The blood red cloth hanging in the window saved Rahab and her household from death. So Christ too shed His blood and hung on the cross to save us from death.

Pneumatology

A consistent stream of the Holy Spirit's work flows throughout the book of Joshua. The work of the Holy Spirit was the same then as it is now; He brings the people into a saving relationship with God and accomplishes the purposes of the Father. His objective in Joshua was the salvation of Israel; for it was through the nation that God chose to save the world (Isaiah 63:7-9).

1. **The Holy Spirit's work is continual** 1:5. He is committed to accomplish the task, no matter how long it takes. His continued presence is necessary for the success of God's plan in the lives of men.

2. **The Holy Spirit's work is mutual** 1:7. Without Him, we cannot; without us, He will not (He can). Cooperation with the Holy Spirit is essential to victory. He empowers us to fulfill our calling and complete the task at hand.

3. **The Holy Spirit's work is supernatural.** The fall of Jericho was wrought by the miraculous destruction of its walls 6:20. Victory was attained at Gibeon when the spirit stayed the sun. 10:12,13.

Out Line

1. Conquest of the land - 1:1-12:24

    i.   Preparation for war - 1:1-5:12
    ii. Conquest 5:13-12:24

2. Division of the Land 13:1-21:45

3. Consecration for continued blessing 22:1-24:33

    i.   Consecration of the Eastern tribes 22:1-34
    ii. Consecration of the Western tribes 23:1-24:28
    iii. Death and burial of Joshua and Eleazer 24:29-33

The overall lesson of the book of Joshua is the imperative of obedience to God, especially in the face of human difficulty.

Application

The faithful meditation of His Word and faithful obedience to His commands are the keys to blessing and abundance (1:8). God hates sin and is just as faithful to punish the disobedient as He is to bless the steadfast. Joshua's life and leadership demonstrated that spiritual maturity is not independent from God, but the responsive dependence on God. To be victorious, we must surrender to Him, to lead others we must follow Him.

JUDGES

The book of Judges traces the history of Israel from the death of Joshua to the beginning of the monarchy, as unstable period of about 350 years. While Joshua is primarily a record of the victory of God's people interspersed with defeat, Judges is a book of defeats punctuated by a few victories.

After the death of Joshua, God rose leaders (called 'judges') to rule the Israelites in peace and drive out enemies still residing in isolated pockets of Canaan. But, unfortunately, the people of Israel rejected God's help and wanted to be totally independent of His interference (21:25). God punished this national attitude by means of national defeat, and when the people finally repented, He forgave them and restored the land to peace.

Authorship and Date

The reporter for this book is unknown, although it is likely that Samuel, the main biblical character to follow, may have written it. This book was probably composed sometime after the death of its last primary character, Samson, around 1051 B. C.

Purpose

Judges reports a repeated cycle of sin, judgment, and repentance salvation. It chronicles the stormy relationship between the Israelites and their God. Two most important truths has been illustrated in this book

1. The desperate sickness of the human heart.
2. God's long-suffering patience, love and mercy.

Theme

Sin grieves and angers God, and carries within itself its own consequences. Repentance secures a loving and merciful response from God and a willingness to restore fellowship.

The Judges

The word 'judges' means one who decides or renders a verdict. The judges were those who ruled or set things right. They delivered people from their oppressors. The judges were civil and political leaders and military champions. They were gallant fighters against heavy odds. They came to the office of judges by the Lord's doing. The Lord's Spirit gifted them. They had the spark of leadership. They were empowered by the Lord (3:10, 6:34, 15:14). These judges were not elected. They moved to the front because the Lord's Spirit was in them. They were simple people with special power and anointing of the Holy Spirit.

Christology

In righteousness, the Lord punished the people of God for their sin; but in His love and mercy, He delivered them in response to their penitent cry. Human kind's need of a divine deliverer or saviour is emphasized in the book of Judges. Throughout history, God's people have sinned. God, as the Lord of history, has always delivered them from oppression when they repented and turned their hearts towards Him. In the fullness of time, God in His love sent forth His Son Jesus Christ as our deliverer, our saviour to redeem us from the bondage of sin and death. Our Lord is the righteous judge (II Tim. 4:8).

Pneumatology

The activity of the Holy Spirit in the book of Judges is clearly portrayed in charismatic leadership of period.

1. The Spirit of the Lord came upon Othniel (3:10) and enabled him to deliver the Israelites from the hand of Cusha-Rishathaim.

2. Through the personal presence of the Holy Spirit Gideon (6:34) delivered God's people from the oppression of the Midianites.

3. The Spirit of the Lord equipped Jephthah (11:29) with leadership skills in his military pursuit against the Ammonites.

4. The Spirit of the Lord empowered Samson to perform extra ordinary deeds (14:6,9).

Out Line

Apostasies of God's People

1. Background 1:1-3:6

    i.   Israel's failure 1:1-2:5
    ii. God's dealings 2:6-3:6

2. History of the Judges (oppression and deliverance) 3:7-16:31

3. Double Appendix (17:1-21:25)

    i.   Idolatry of Dan 17:1-18:31
    ii. Immortality of Benjamin 19: 1-21:25

Application

There are disastrous consequences of breaking fellowship with God through idolatrous worship. Sin separates us from God. If we repent, He restores the fellowship again. God is able to empower us with His Holy Spirit and to use us to bring deliverance to those who are bound in sin and despair. He responds to the cry of a penitent heart. The Lord is faithful and His love is constant.

RUTH

In the tumultuous years of the judges, an era marked mainly by deceit, rebellion and war, shines a woman of character, integrity, and consecration to God, Ruth, a gentile, married to a Hebrew. Ruth is a Moabite widow, who leaves her homeland to travel and reside with her widowed mother – in – law, Naomi. 'Ruth' is a story of devotion and faithfulness, pure love and loyalty, characteristics strangely absent from the pages of Judges.

Authorship and Date

We are unsure as to who wrote Ruth, however the original author is God Himself. The book may have been written sometime during the reign of King David, 1011-971 B. C.

Purpose

The book of Ruth does show the shallowness and selfishness of Jewish particularism. It definitely teaches that the true people of God are any who choose to follow Him, not the members of a certain nation or group. The primary purpose of this book is also to tell something about the ancestry of King David.

Theme and Theology

The grace of God extends to all who exercise faith. The Lord's providential care. He is clearly at work in the lives of those open to Him. The Lord's grace and care are not limited by national or racial boundaries. God is watching over His people, and that He brings to God what is good. This book is a book about God. He rules over all and brings blessing to those who trust Him.

Christology

Boaz foreshadows the redeeming work of Jesus Christ. The role of the "kinsman – redeemer" is beautifully fulfilled in Boaz's actions bringing about Ruth's personal restoration. By His willingness to identify with the human family (as Boaz assumed the duties of his human family), Christ has worked a thorough – going redemption of our plight. Further, Ruth's inability to do anything to alter her estate, typifies absolute human helplessness (Rom. 5:6) and Boaz's willingness to pay the complete price (4:9) foreshadows Christ's full payment for our salvation (I Cor. 6:20, Gal. 3:13, I Pet. 1:18,19).

Pneumatology

There is no direct reference to the Holy Spirit in this book. However, Naomi stands as the type of Holy Spirit. Naomi is seen as a gracious and tender woman who navigates great difficulties with an abiding fidelity.

Out Line

1. To Moab and return 1:1-22

2. God's gracious provision 2:1-23
3. A claim to kinship 3:1-18
4. The kinsman – redeemer 4:1-17
5. Conclusion 4:18-22

Application

The inclusion of the Moabites, Ruth, as a Gentile participant in Israel's kingly line, pictures God's love as it reaches out to all the nations of the world. The book of Ruth ennobles the beauty of commitment and fellowship and underscores the value of family commitment. Ruth's prioritizing is the lesson for all of us today.

Ruth

The meaning of the word is "friendship". Naomi and her husband went to live in Moab the time of famine in Israel. After the famine was over, Naomi's husband died, and she wanted to return home. Ruth, a Moabite woman was married to Naomi's son, but he also died. Now Ruth and Naomi had only each other to love. So, Ruth left her own country to return to Israel with her mother–in–law. As they started back to Bethlehem, Ruth showed her love to Naomi by vowing never to leave her.

When the two widows arrived in Bethlehem, it was harvest time. To get food, Ruth arranged to work as a gleaner-one who picked up what the threshes dropped or left in the fields. She worked for Boaz, a relative of Naomi. Boaz saw the young widow working hard in the field and began asking questions about her. Eventually, Boaz and Ruth were married and had a son- Obed whom Naomi helped care for.

Ruth stayed in Israel, accepting the country as her own. She was the great- grand mother of King David and listed in Matt. 1:5 as one of the ancestors of Jesus.

I AND II SAMUEL

The books of Samuel are significant books. They cover a period of more than 100 years from the prayer for Samuel, through most of the reign of David. They document the change in leadership from Judges to Kings.

Authorship and Date

Like all the historical books of the Old Testament from Joshua to Esther, this book is anonymous. It is possible that Samuel was its author and wrote between 1025-900 B. C.

Purpose

The books of Samuel were written to present a connected history of the events surrounding the establishment of the monarchy. They deal with the last Judges and introduce the first two Kings during this vital transition period. Samuel's ministry as a prophet is also of importance for understanding the development of the prophetic office as well as the later work of leading prophets. The moral and spiritual lessons inherent in the experience of Samuel, Saul, David and others are of timeless value.

Theme

God is merciful and patient always desiring to keep His people. Although He commissions and calls men to shepherd and lead His people, they do not always remain faithful to His call.

When the Spirit of God is in control of a person's heart, blessing and success results. But when selfish desires are in control, it results in punishment and failure.

Theology

a.   The will of God

b.   The doctrine of sin. Both I and II Samuel illustrates all too vividly the sinfulness of the human heart and the inevitable results of sin. The experience of David provides the greatest instruction both positively and negatively. When David acknowledged his sin, the Lord forgave and restored spiritually (II Sam. 12:13).

c.   The Davidic covenant.

Christology

The similarities between Jesus and the boy Samuel are striking. Both were the children of promise. Both were dedicated to God before birth. Both were the bridges of transition from one stage of the nation's history to another. In David, the earthly lineage of God's Kingdom begins. In Christ, God comes as King and will come again as King of Kings. David, the simple shepherd boy, prefigures Christ, the good shepherd. Jesus becomes the ultimate shepherd – King. His combination of the office of prophet, priest and king- David is a forerunner of the root of Jesse, Jesus Christ.

Pneumatology

This book contains remarkable instances of the coming of the Holy Spirit upon the prophet, as well as upon Saul and his servants. In 10:6, the Holy Spirit comes upon Saul, who prophesies and is turned into another man, that is, equipped by the Spirit to fulfill God's calling.

Jesus explained the work of the Spirit in John 16:8, when He has come, He will convict the world of sin and of righteousness and of judgment. The convicting or convincing work of the Spirit is seen clearly with Nathan, the prophet confronting David about sin with Bethsheba and Urriah. David's sin is laid bare, righteousness is accomplished and the judgment is spelled out.

Out Line

1. Samuel and the reign of Saul I Sam. 1-14
    i.   The ministry of Samuel I Sam. 1-7
    ii. The initial years of Saul's reign I Sam. 8:14

2. The rise of David to the throne I Sam. 15- II Sam. 8
    i. David's struggle with King Saul I Sam. 15-31
    ii. David's unification of Judah and Israel II Sam. 1-8

3. Problems in the reign of David – II Sam. 9-20

4. Conclusion- II Sam. 21-24.

Application

God is at work in history. Even the most sinful and rebellious occurrences can be used by Him to continue His divine plan. God steps into the pain and misery of Hannah to give her, children (2:21). Though men look at the outward appearance, God looks at the heart (16:7). Obedience is better than men's hearts as well as their actions. God is the God of patience and forgiveness. God has left the church in the world as the Body of Christ to witness for Him and to carry out His purposes on the earth today.

I AND II KINGS

I and II Kings describes the kings of Israel's monarchy from the closing days of the rule of David until the time of the Babylonian exile. After an extensive account of Solomon's reign, the narrative records the division of the kingdom and presents an interrelated picture of developments within the two kingdoms.

Four keys milestone of the events

(i)   The beginning of the rule by kings (Saul, David and Solomon)
(ii) The split of the kingdom in Israel (North and Judah)
(iii) Israel captured by Assyrian in 722 BC.
(iv) Judah captured by Babylon in 586 BC.

Authorship and Date

We don't know who wrote it. Anyway the author was a Jewish captive in Babylon, like Jeremiah, probably wrote between 562-536 BC.

Purpose

Following are the purpose of I and II Kings:

(1) To show how God blessed those kings who obeyed Him and honored His house. Those who did well were blessed.

(2) To show how the kingdom was divided and taken away in fulfillment of prophecy.

(3) To demonstrate God's faithfulness in fulfilling His promise to David to establish His house and His throne forever (II Sam. 7 : 12- 17).

Theme

The blessing of God promised to those who obey. A nation that rejects God is also rejected by God. This is what the theme of I and II Kings is all about.

Christology

The failure of the prophets, priests and kings of God's people points to the necessity of the advent of Christ. Christ Himself would be the ideal combination of these three offices. As a prophet, Christ and word far surpassed the great prophet Elijah (Matt. 17:1-5). Christ is a Priest superior to any of those recorded in Kings (Heb. 7: 22-27). Christ is the King greater than their greatest king (Matt. 12 : 42). The reign of each of the 26 rulers came to an end, but Christ will reign on the throne of David forever (I Chr. 17 : 14, I Sam. 9 : 6)

Pneumatology

There is an allusion in 18:46 (the hand of the Lord) to the Holy Spirit's work of enabling Elijah to do the miracles. The formula *'hand of the Lord'* referred to the inspiration of the prophets by the Spirit of God. Here, the hand of the Lord, refers to the Spirit of God who endowed Elijah with supernatural strength to do amazing things.

There is an indirect reference to the Holy Spirit in the phrase "Spirit of Elijah" found in 2:9. Here Elisha is seeking to receive the same empowerment, Elijah had, in order to carry on Elijah's prophetic ministry. The energizing Spirit or power that enabled Elijah to prophesy was the Spirit of God. II Kings 2:9-16 then provides an interesting Old Testament parallel to Acts 1:4-9 and 2:1-4.

Out Line

1. The Solomonic era (I Kings 1:1-12:24)
2. Israel and Judah from Jeroboam/Rehoboam-Ahab/ Ase 12:25- 16:34
3. The ministries of Elijah and Elisha and other prophets, from Ahad/Asa- Joram/Johoshaphat (I Kings 17:1- II Kings 8:15)
4. Israel and Judah from Joram/ Jehoram to the exile of Israel (II Kings 8:16-17:41)
5. Judah from Hezekiah to the Babylonian exile (II Kings 18-25)

Application

God still controls human affairs. The nation, leader or person who responds to and obeys the Lord's will enjoys the benefits of a relationship with Him. Those who refuse and rebel will experience God's discipline. Though people are sinful, God is the author of redemption and He graciously forgives those who repent and return to Him.

I AND II CHRONICLES

The books focus specially on the Southern Kingdom of Judea in general and the line of David in particular, covering the period of Jewish history from the reign of David to the Babylonian captivity. The books stress the critical value of pure worship of the one true God of Israel. Whereas David is the central figure of I Chronicles, his descendent occupy center stage in II Chronicles.

Chronicles was written for the exiled Jews in Babylon, preparing to return to their homeland (II Chron. 36:22,23).

Authorship and Date

The author of these books is unknown. There is a possibility that they were penned by the scribe Ezra, between 450 – 425 B.C.

Purpose

The two books are an assurance to those in captivity, that God is still interested in them and loves them. God will restore and forgive those who repent of their sins and worship Him in faithfulness and truth.

Theme

Chronicler wrote these books for the restored community. God can restore His wandering people, even though they were often complaining and grumbling.

Christology

In I Chronicle 21, David buys a piece of property from Ornan on which to make a sacrifice that stops the plague. This site on mount Moriah was the very place where Solomon would build the temple (3:1). It is possible that this was the very mountain where Abraham was asked to sacrifice his son (Gen. 22:2). In the New Testament, three times Paul refers to believers as a temple of God (I Cor. 3:16, 17, 6:19; Eph. 2:19-22). It is Christ who has purchased the ground for this spiritual temple. It was His sacrifice that delivered us from death (Rom. 5:12-18, 7:24,25; I Jn. 3: 14).

Pneumatology

There are two clear references to the Holy Spirit in this book. The Spirit came upon Amasai and enabled him to give an inspired utterance (12:18). The second reference is that, it was through the ministry of the Spirit that the plans of the temple were revealed to David. (28:12).

A picture of the Holy Spirit is seen in II Chron. 5:13, 14 at the dedication of the temple. This temple, which was built on a place that was purchased, a place where sacrifice was made for sin, is now filled with the presence of God. In the New Testament, Paul explains that believers are the temple of God, the dwelling place of the Holy Spirit. (I Cor. 3:16,6:19).

Out Line

1. Genealogies: Creation to restoration (I Chron. 1-9)
2. The reign of David (I Chron. 10-29)
3. The reign of Solomon (II Chron. 1-9)
4. The Schism and the history of kings of Judah (II Chron. 10-36)

Application

God has been faithful throughout history to deliver those who cry out to Him. It is the great source of encouragement that God is a promise-making and promise keeping God who is worthy to be trusted. He is still a God of hope. His purposes will prevail in the lives of His people. We have to learn from the failure of God's people in the past, in order that we ought not make the same mistakes (I Cor. 10:11, Heb 4:11).

EZRA

It is the first of the post captivity books (Ezra, Nehemiah, Esther, Haggai, Zechariah and Malachi) which records the return to Palestine under Zerubbabal, by decree of Cyrus, of Jewish remnant who laid the temple foundation (BC. 536). Later (BC. 458) Ezra followed and restored most of the princes, remained by preference in Babylon and Assyria, where they were prospering. The post captivity books deal with that feeble remnant which alone had a heart for God.

Authorship and Date

Ezra may have written this book soon after returning to Jerusalem from Babylon, around 450BC.

Purpose

This book is an excellent documentation of God's fulfillment of His promises of restoration through the prophet Isaiah and Jeremiah.

Theme

God is faithful to His promises. God uses whoever suits His purpose, whether Cyrus and Artaxerxes or Ezra, Zerubbabal and Nehemiah. God empowered His chosen people to overcome all opposition, even against impossible odds.

Christology

Ezra himself foreshadows Christ by his life and work;

(i)   As one who had prepared his heart to seek the law of the Lord and to do it (7:10, is parallel to Jn. 5:19).

(ii) As the priest (7:11), Ezra foreshadows Christ' role as the great High Priest (Heb. 4:14).

(iii) As the great spiritual reformer who calls Israel to repentance (Ch 10), Ezra typifies Christ' Messianic role as the reshaper of Israel's spiritual perspectives, including a call away from dead traditionalism and moral impurity (Matt. 11:20-24, 23).

Pneumatology

The working of the Holy Spirit in Ezra is clealry seen in the providential moving of God to fulfill His promises. This is indicated by the phrase 'the hand of the Lord'. Moreover, the work of the Holy Spirit is clearly seen in Ezra's personal life, both in terms of working in him (7:10) and on his behalf (7:6).

Out Line

1. Restoration under the governor: Zerubbabal (1:1-6:22)
    (i)   The journey (1:1-2:70)
    (ii) The task: Rebuilding the temple (3:1-6:22)

2. Reforms under the priest: Ezra (7:1-10:44)
    (i)   The journey (7:1-8:32)

(ii) The task: Dissolving mixed marriages (8:33-10:44).

Application

Erring saints cannot totally thwart God's sovereign plans, but they can delay or frustrate them. God is greater than us, and He does not have ways of transcending or shortcomings. However, He wants us to walk in obedience so that His plans can be fulfilled as originally revealed.

NEHEMIAH

The book of Nehemiah begins its story twelve years after the narrative of Ezra closes. Nehemiah, cup bearer to the Persian King, Artaxerxes, led a small third expedition to Jerusalem to assist his brethren in the task of rebuilding the walls of the city. In biblical times, a city without a wall was an open invitation to thieves and enemies.

Authorship and Date

The book is named after its chief character and author. It opens with a clear statement of authorship, "The words of Nehemiah son of Hacaliah" (1:1). This book was written around the time the walls were reconstructed, 420 BC.

Purpose

The book continue the theme of Ezra, namely preserving the truth of God's enduring faithfulness to His promises to His people.

Theme

Sin is the spiritual disease which damages the entire being. God can restore the damage done by sin.

Christology

Nehemiah was a courageous leader, defying the odds and encouraging the people to do God's work (2:18), even as Christ defied the people's opposition and encouraged His disciples to endure (John 15:18-27).

Pneumatology

Since creation, the Holy Spirit has been the executive arm of God on earth. The hand of God (2:18), His action on earth, is the Holy Spirit. Nehemiah whose name means '*Yahweh Comforts*' was clearly an instrument of the Holy Spirit. Under the power of God's Spirit, he certainly modeled the Holy Spirit working and became one of the early fulfillments of this remarkable prophecy.

Out Line

1. The work 1:1-7:73a
   i. Planned 1:1-3:32
   ii. Threatened 4:1-6:14
   iii. Finished 6:15-7:73a

2. The worship 7:73b-13: 31
   i. Revival 7:73b-10: 39
   ii. Redistribution 11:1-12:26
   iii. Rededication 12:27-43
   iv. Reform 12:44-13:31

Application

Four lasting principles stand out in the book of Nehemiah :

(1) **Compassion** is often the springboard of obedience to God's will.

(2) **Cooperation** with others is required to carry out God's will.

(3) **Confidence** results from fervent prayers and the exposition of the Word of God, which reveals God's will.

(4) **Courage** will manifest itself as sanctified tenacity in refusing to compromise on the conviction that one is doing God's will.

ESTHER

Esther was a devout Jewish orphan maiden who lived in Shushan, Persia's principal city. She was nurtured by the cousin, Mordecai, who was an official in the palace of king Xerxes. After the king had divorced his wife, he selects a new wife. His choice? Esther. This made her the queen over an enormous empire.

Authorship and Date

Although Esther is the main character of the book, it is unlikely that she was the author. Perhaps Ezra or Nehemiah wrote this parenthetical account sometime around 483-473 B.C.

Purpose

The major purpose of the book of Esther is to show how a host of Jews living in exile were spared by means of a Gentile king, from well-planned extermination.

Theme

The fate of all nations good or bad- is in the sovereign hands of God. Though the name of God never appears in this book, God's power is implied everywhere in the book. The book of Esther teaches that God's providence is active in every facet of human life. We cannot escape Him. His purposes, though sometimes hidden, are far-reaching. We can be confident of God's care and protection.

Christology

Queen Esther typifies Jesus. She lived in submission, dependence and obedience to her God given authorities, as Christ did. Esther also fully identified herself with her people and fasted for three days, as she interceded to God on their behalf (4:16) parallel to Matt. 4:2 and John 17: 20. Finally Esther gave up her right to live in order to save the nation from certain death. For this, she was exalted by the king which is similar to Jesus', humanity in Phil. 2:5-11.

Pneumatology

Although the Holy Spirit is not mentioned directly, it is His work that produced the deep level of humanity in both Esther and Mordecai, leading to their mutual love and loyalty. The Holy Spirit also directed and energized Esther to fast for her nation and to call her people to do the same.

Out Line

A story of providential care

1. Jews are threatened 1:1-3:15
    (i) The setting 1:1-2:23
    (ii) The plot 3:1-15

2. The Jews are spared 4:1-10:3
    (i) Deliverance 4:1-9:16
    (ii) Commemoration 9:17-32
    (iii) Exaltation 10:1-3

The book of Esther is a study of the survival of God's people amidst hostility. Esther and Mordecai play the central role in this book. Esther, spiritual maturity is seen in her knowing to wait for God's timing to make her request to save her people and to denounce Haman (5:6-8). Mordecai also demonstrates a maturity to seek God for timing and direction. Both Esther and Mordecai feared God, not men. Both of them played an important part in saving the life of the people that the enemy planned to destroy. As a result, they led a nation into freedom, were honored by king and given greater authority, privileges and responsibilities.

Application

The book of Esther is the classical example of successful teamwork: Esther and Mordecai. If we are united we will make (build) up, if divided fall down. God will destroy those who try to harm God's people.

POETICAL BOOKS

From Job to the Song of Solomon, the books contain the poetical devices. The language which is used in these books is highly poetical.

Not only that, the different metaphors and similes are used. Due to these various elements of poetry, these books are known as the poetical books in the Old Testament.

JOB

The Old Testament book about Job is one of the supreme offerings of the human mind to the living God and one of the best gifts of God to men. The book of Job is about the unchanging human realities-war, destitution, sickness, humiliation, and depression. Also the unchanging goodness of God, who transform our human agony into justice, kindness, love and joy. It is the story of a man who held on to his life to God, with a faith that survived the torments of utter loss and expanded into new realms of wonder and delight.

Authorship and Date

The actual author is not identified. We may be sure that he was an Israelite, since he frequently uses the Israelite covenant name for God (Yahweh). Date of the writing appears to be from 2000-1000 BC. This book was written to the people of Israel. It was probably written in or near Uz, the country where Job lived, east of the Jordan River.

Purpose

The main purpose of this book is to encourage God's people to remain faithful to Him, even during difficult times and to trust Him, even when it is hard to understand His purposes. The book portrays both man's faith in God and God's faith in man.

Theme

Trust in God is based on confidence in his character (who) rather than an explanation for our circumstances (why). The problem of the suffering of righteous persons is the major theme of the book. Nevertheless, Job remains primarily a book about faith. It probes both the dark and bright sides of faith – the agonizing struggle and the inspiring triumph of trust and hope.

Christology

Job may be seen as a type of Christ. Job suffered greatly and was humbled and stripped of all he had, but in the end he was restored and became the intercessor for his friends. Christ emptied Himself, taking on Himself a human form. He suffered, was persecuted by men and demons, seemed forsaken by God and became an intercessor. Job was compelled by situation but Jesus chose to suffer.

Pneumatology

The Holy Spirit in the book of Job is the Creator and Sustainer of life and He gives meaning and rationality (wisdom) to life. God is neither capricious nor selfish. Because He cares for man, He constantly sustains him by the abundant flow of His Spirit. Knowledge and wisdom are the Spirit's gift to men. He is also the source of life itself (33:4). The Spirit of God is the Spirit of life.

Out Line

1. Prologue (Ch. 1-2)

    i.   Job's happiness (1:1-5)
    ii. Job's testing (1:6-2:13)

2. Dialogue – Dispute (Ch. 3-27)

    i.   Job's opening lament (Ch.3)
    ii. First cycle of speeches (Ch.4-14)
    iii. Second cycle of speeches (Ch.15-21)
    iv. Third cycle of speeches (Ch.22-26)
    v. Job's closing discourse (Ch.27)

3. Interlude on wisdom (Ch. 28)

4. Monologues (29:1-42:6)

    i.   Job's call for vindication (Ch.29-31)
    ii. Elihu's speeches (Ch.32-37)
    iii. Divine discourses (38:1-42:6)

5. Epilogue (42:7-17)

    i.   God's verdict (42:7-9)

ii.   Job's restoration (42:10-17)

The Message of Job for Today

i.   For most people, life consists of a series of ups and downs.
     Sometimes life seems too good to be true; at other times the
     sorrows and pain seem unbearable. Earthly existence holds no
     guarantee of a trial-free life.

ii. The problem of innocent suffering still looms in the world.

iii. Reward and restoration will eventually come to those who trust
     in the Lord. Life must remain a pilgrimage of faith for the
     righteous sufferer till his time.

Application

(1) God is sovereign. We cannot understand His working by
     rational thinking alone. Faith is needed.

(2) We understand ourselves and our lives in direct relationship
     to our understanding of the character and workings of God.

(3) The struggle of faith is a personal one. We enter the crucible of
     life alone, we must test the mettle of our faith in God against
     uncontrollable forces and win our individual victories. There
     will be times when family and friends may be taken from us
     and we must stand alone.

PSALMS

The entire collection of Psalms is entitled 'Praises' in the
Hebrew texts.

Authorship and Date

There are more than 7 composers. King David wrote at least 75 of
the 15 Psalms; the son of Korah 10 (42, 44-49, 84, 85, 87),
Asaph 12 (50, 73-83), Solomon (72, 127), Moses (90), Heman (88)
and Ethan (89). The remaining 48 Psalms remain anonymous in
their authorship, although Ezra is thought to be the author of it. The
time range of the Psalms extends from Moses (1410 BC) to the late
6th or early 5th century BC, postexilic period (126), which spans
about 900 years of Jewish history.

Purpose

i.   To reveal God and the way to worship and walk with Him.

ii. To inspire, challenge, comfort and transform everyone, who encounters them.

iii. To show the reality of human existence and God's glory.

Theme

God is worthy of our adoration and praises. The basic theme of Psalms is living real life in the real world, where two dimensions (horizontal and vertical) operate simultaneously. Without denying the pain of the horizontal dimension, the people of God are to live joyfully and dependently on the person and promises standing behind the vertical dimension. All cycles of human troubles and triumphs provide occasions for expressing human complaints, confidence, prayers or praise, to Israel's sovereign Lord.

Types of Psalms

i.   **Individual and communal lament**: 3-7, 12, 13, 22, 25-28, 35, 38-40, 42-44, 51, 54-57, 59-61, 63-64, 69-71, 74, 79-80, 83, 85, 86, 88, 90, 102, 109, 120, 123, 130, 140-143.

ii.   **Thanksgiving**: 8, 18, 19, 29-30, 32-34, 36, 40, 41, 66, 103-106, 111, 113, 116, 117, 124, 129, 135, 136, 138, 139, 146-148, 150.

iii. **Enthronement**: 47, 93, 96-99

iv.   **Pilgrimage**: 43, 46, 48, 76, 84, 87, 120-134.

v.   **Royal**: 2, 18, 20, 21, 45, 72, 89, 101, 110, 132, 144.

vi.   **Wisdom**: 1, 37, 119.

vii. **Imprecatory**: 7, 35, 40, 55, 58, 59, 69, 79, 109, 137, 139, 144.

Christology

About half of the Old Testament references to the Messiah[13] quoted

---

[13] Messiah is the hellenized transliteration of the Aramaic *mesiha*. The underlying Hebrew word is derived from the verb '*masah*', that means to anoint, smear with oil. The ancient custom of consecrating priests, prophets and kings by anointing them with oil lead to the description of such persons as anointed ones (Messiahs). The promised seed of the woman, the virgin

by New Testament writers are from this book. Some of the prophetic references to Christ are typical, that is, symbolic shadows of future realities. Other references are direct prophetic statements. The apostles saw prophetic reference in this book to Christ's birth (Acts 13:33), His lineage (Matt. 22:42, 43), His zeal (John 2:17), His teaching by parables (Matt. 13:35), His vicarious suffering (Rom.15:3), His resurrection (Acts 2:25-28), ascension (Acts 2:34) and reign (I Cor. 15:27).

Pneumatology

The Psalms are unique and vastly different from the works of secular composers. Both may reflect the depths of agony experienced by the tormented human spirit, with all its pathos, and express the rapturous joy of the freed soul, yet Psalms moves to a higher plane by the creative anointing of the Holy Spirit.

Application

The Psalms have been a source of personal inspiration and spiritual strength. In the course of dealing with adversities of life, people are often frustrated by not being able to express adequately their emotional pain or mental anguish. The Psalms release us from that frustration. By song and spirit, they comfort the lonely, strengthen the weary, bind the broken - hearted, and turn the eyes of the downcast up towards their Creator. Hope returns, faith is renewed, and life again becomes bearable.

PROVERBS

Proverbs belongs to the general class of wisdom literature. The wisdom literature is the philosophical literature of the Hebrews. It is concerned with the proper governance of life through an understanding of ultimate goals and general principles.

---

born Christ (Gen. 3: 15, Isa. 7: 14), held the three offices of Prophet, Priest and King and was thus the Messiah par excellence. So, Jesus Christ is the Messiah of God (Rom. 1 :4 ; Phil. 2 : 9 - 11). Other messianic titles attributed to Jesus include Servant, Lord, Son of God, the King, the Holy One, the Righteous One and Judge.

Authorship and Date
The entire book of Proverbs was written by Solomon, sometimes between 950-900 BC.

Purpose
The main purpose of the Proverbs is to provide a text book for the moral guidance and intellectual growth of youth and at the same time serve as a source of study and inspiration for the spiritually mature (1:2-3).

Theme
True wisdom is built upon an acknowledgement of God for who He is. Wisdom is the main theme of the Proverbs. Wisdom is God's gift to those dedicated to morality. The word wisdom is used in different ways.

i.   Instruction or training (1:2,3)
ii. Understanding or insight (2:2)
iii. Wise dealing (10:5, 12:8)
iv. Shrewdness (1:40) and discretion (1:4b)
v.   Words of knowledge and learning (1:5)

This wisdom is costly which comes only after
i.   Conversion: A turning from evil (9:10). Turning from darkness wickedness to the light.

     (Come...eat...drink...forsake...live...walk (9:5-6).

ii. Devotion: Wisdom is for the humbly eager.

Christology
The book performs a powerful service in whetting the human appetite for wisdom and understanding, a hunger that can only be fully satisfied in Christ. Point by point, the qualities of wisdom are the qualities of Christ. Obedience to God, right behavior, patience, and reliability, humility all these plus love is perfectly illustrated in the savior.

Pneumatology

The Holy Spirit is not mentioned directly in the book. But wisdom refers to the Spirit (1:23), which, of course, is the Spirit of God. In fact, a main point of the book is that wisdom apart from God is impossible, so in that sense this Spirit is prominent throughout the book.

Out Line

1. Title, introduction and motto (1:1-7)
2. A Father's praise of wisdom (1:8-9:18)
3. Proverbs of Solomon (10:1-22:16)
4. Words of wise men (22:17-24:34)
5. Further proverbs of Solomon (25:1-29:27)
6. Words of Agur (30:1-33)
7. Words of King Lemuel (31:1-9)
8. An alphabet of wifely excellence (31:10-31)

Application

The book of Proverbs contains wisodom. It tells how to order one's values, which leads to character, wholeness and satisfaction. It warns about the pitfalls along the way, and declares the folly of not developing the fear of the Lord. It is ever relevent for every area of life.

ECCLESIASTES

The name *'ecclesiastes'* in the Latin and English Bible comes from the Greek word for assembly or congregation, *ekklesia*. So, this book is the book of the teacher or the preacher. He is the leader or speaker in the assembly. It has been called by somebody as *'the journal of a desperate man'*. The author records a seemingly endless list of pursuits; pleasures and pondering of a life lived apart from God.

Authorship and Date

Though not specifically named, Solomon is commonly recognized as the author of this book because of the extensive list of personal experiences outlined in it, he probably wrote this book during his later years, around 900 BC.

Purpose

The main purpose of this book is to show how futile and useless it is to pursue materialistic, selfish, earthly goals as ends in themselves, and to point to God, as the only source of lasting personal fulfillment and meaning.

Theme

Life is meaningless apart from God, the author of life. Life is perplexing, nature contradictory and existence wearing. God is 'up there' somewhere, but He is remote and has chosen to relate to people only from a distance. Ultimate values are few and far between. The best one can do is to live one's life day by day, enjoying the simple pleasures, and trying not to claim greater knowledge of God that is available. Vanity under sun but hope in God.

Christology

Although the book contains no direct or typological prophecies of Jesus Christ, it anticipates a number of teachings of Him who was the fulfillment of the law and the prophets. In Matt. 6:19-21, Jesus warned against seeking wealth in life, urging instead that it be sought in the next, a perspective that echoes the preachers indictment of materialism in 2:1-11, 18-26, 4:4-6, 5:8-14, and so on.

Pneumatology

All references of the Spirit in this book are the life force that animates the human or the animal (3:18-21). The book nevertheless anticipates some of the problems faced by the apostle Paul in the implementation of the spiritual gifts in I Cor. 12-14.

Out Line

1. Introduction 1:1-11
2. 1st Sermon: Purpose with God 1:12-3:15
3. 2nd Sermon: Worship of God 3:16-5:20
4. 3rd Sermon: Gift from God 6:1-8:13
5. 4th sermon: Knowledge of God 8:14-12:7
6. Conclusion: Fear of God 12:8-14

Application

The determination of the preacher to find what is of real value in this life should be a challenge for any true believer of Jesus Christ (John 14:6). The preacher's failure to find real value in earthly things and comfortable life- style challenges the Christian who lives in this age of greed and materialism to concentrate on the things that are above (Col. 3:1) and not to glorify greed and possessions.

SONG OF SOLOMON

The Song of Solomon is a song of love. First of all, the Song is a book of poems about human, sensual love. They are the songs of a man and woman who care, deeply for one another. Secondly, the Song continues the story of human love that began in the Garden of Eden (naked but feeling no shame). Thirdly, the Song tells us about God and our relationship with Him, but not directly, since God's name never occurs in the book.

Authorship and Date

Solomon is the author by his own statement (1:1). It seems that it was written to the author's lover, whether real or figurative. It was written probably around 10th century BC.

Purpose

1.   Didactic

It is didactic and moral in its purpose. Despite their passion and desire for each other, they observe purity and apply self-restraint. They reserve sex for marriage. Thus, they demonstrate how holiness can be maintained in this sinful world, where love and lust are often mixed.

2.   Celebration of human intimacy

Biblically, the most intimate knowledge of another person is in the sexual relationship of a man and a woman. It is a way to know each other emotionally and spiritually.

Christology

The Garden of Eden, the promised land, the tabernacle with its ark of the covenant, the temple of Solomon, the new heavens and the new earth are all related to Jesus Christ. The very essence of covenant history and covenant love is reproduced in Him (Luke 24:27, II Cor. 1:20).

Pneumatology

The Holy Spirit is the bond and the binding power of love. The joyous oneness revealed in the Song is inconceivable apart from the Holy Spirit. The very form of the book as Song and symbol is especially adapted to the Spirit, for He Himself uses dream, picture language and singing (Act 2:17, Eph. 5: 18,19).

Out Line

1. Title 1:1
2. Courtship day's 1:2-3:5
3. Wedding 3:6-5:1
4. Married life 5:2-8:14
5. Troubles dream of separation 5:2-6:3
6. Mutual love of husband and wife 6:4-8:4
7. The seal of their love 8:5-14

Application

The Song is a constant goad to drifting marriages with its challenge to seek for openness, growth and joyous relationship. As a biblical archetype, it can bring healing to the core of our being with its hope of covenant love as it reshapes our marriages. Its portrayal of the covenant love relationship also applies to the covenant love relationship enjoyed by God's church.

PROPHETICAL BOOKS

The Writing Prophets

Priest is a spokesman of man who speaks to God on behalf of man; prophet is a spokesman of God who speaks to man on behalf of God. There are 17 prophetical books. There are 5 major prophets and 12 minor prophets. Major prophets are called so because of the relative length, not importance, of their prophesy.

Three Periods of the Prophets

1. Pre – exilic prophets – 11 prophets ministered during the years leading up to the Assyrian captivity of the northern kingdom (722 BC) and the Babylonian captivity of the southern kingdom (586 BC)

i. Assyrian captivity
    Israel – Amos and Hosea

ii. Babylonian captivity
     Judah – Nahum, Zephaniah, Jeremiah, Habakkuk

iii. Three earlier prophets

     Israel – Jonah
     Judah – Obadiah and Joel

2. Exilic prophets – Daniel and Ezekiel

3. Post – exilic prophets – Zechariah, Haggai and Malachi (the final voice from God until John the Baptist)

We live in a chaotic world. Chaos reigns within nations. Chaos reigns among nations. Hatredness, self – seeking, social injustice, the abandonment of moral standards, the breakdown of family relationships, all is so dismally familiar. Yet, man holds pride that seems ready to rationalize any type of conduct and excuse any type of evil.

The Old Testament prophets lived in the same chaotic world as we do. They suffered and were questioned, but they saw beyond the confusion of the times to a God of unchanging standards and purpose, a God who is moving towards a glorious end and will settle for nothing less than what He has predestined.

The inspired insights of the prophets offer us answers to our questions. God's answers demand that we face up to ourselves and to Him. Then we will find that there is a God who is in control. There is righteousness to be pursued. There is a sure and glorious hope to be attained.

MAJOR PROPHETS

Isaiah, Jeremiah, Lamentation, Ezekiel and Daniel are known as the major prophetical books of the Old Testament.

ISAIAH

The word Isaiah means salvation of Judah. It is the most quoted Old Testament prophet in the New Testament and also contains the largest number of prophecies surrounding the Messiah, Jesus.

Authorship and Date

Isaiah son of Amoz wrote this book during the reigns of Uzziah, Jotham, Ahaz and Hezekiah, kings of Judah (1:1). Since the time frame in which these kings ruled was 740-690 BC, this book was written during this period.

Purpose

There are mainly threefold purposes of this book-

i.   To speak out against the sin of the people and the impending judgments of God (1-39).

ii. To foretell Judah's captivity by an enemy from the east, the Babylonians (39:6-7).

iii. To predict the first and second comings of the Messiah (40-66) and other events surrounding the end times (65:17).

Theme and Theology

The God of Israel is a holy yet compassionate God. The theological message of the book may be summarized as follows: The Lord will fulfill His ideal for Israel by purifying His people through judgment and then restoring them to a renewed covenantal relationship. He will establish Jerusalem (Zion) as the centre of His worldwide Kingdom and reconcile once hostile nations to Himself.

Christology

Christ is spoken of as the Lord, Immanuel, Wonderful Counselor, Mighty God, Everlasting Father, Prince of Peace, King, Lamb of

God, Redeemer and Anointed One. Chapter 53 is the single greatest Old Testament chapter prophesying the Messiah's atoning work. This chapter sets forth the purpose of Christ's vicarious death on the cross.

Pneumatology

The Holy Spirit is mentioned 15 times in the book, not counting references to His power, effect.

1. The Spirit's anointing upon Messiah is to empower Him for His rule and administration as king on the throne of David (11:1-12).

2. The Spirit's outpouring upon Israel is to give them success in their rehabilitation (44:1-5, 59:19, 21).

3. The Spirit's operation at creation is the preservation of nature (40:13).

Out Line

1. Judgment of the Lord 1:1-39:8

    i. Prophecies of Judah 1:1-12:6
    ii. Prophecies to foreign nations 13:1-23:18
    iii. Warning and promises 24:1-35:10
    iv. History 36:1-39:8

2. Comfort of the Lord 40:1-66:24

    i. Salvation promised: The one true God 40:1-48:22
    ii. Salvation provided: The Messiah 49:1-57:21
    iii.Salvation realized: God in His throne 58:1-66:24

Application

Isaiah focused a spotlight of holiness upon the sordid sins of Israel. He summoned his contemporaries to cease from their social injustice, their quest for carnal indulgence, their trust in the arm of flesh, and their hypocritical pretence of orthodox religion. He also warned of the consequence of Judgment if sin continued. This is relevent even for today and forever.

JEREMIAH

Jeremiah is the book of warning. About 60 years after the death of Isaiah, God raised up another prophet for His people. Jeremiah means 'God sends'. He is known as the weeping prophet. Jeremiah, a young man of 21 years began his ministry when the condition was very critical. The people were far from God and drifting further still. He was God's mouthpiece for about 50 years in all. Most people rejected him and his message but he remained true to his calling. The book ends with the tragic account of Babylonian captivity.

Authorship and Date

Jeremiah was the son of the priest, Hilkiah. He ministered between 627-575 BC. He wrote the various parts of the book, at different times, during this period and from a variety of locations.

Purpose

To warn at all the time about the divine law of reaping what you sow. God's heart breaks over the sin of His children; even in judgment He promises restoration.

Theme and Message

God judges sin and rewards righteousness. Jeremiah brought a message of judgment against the people of Israel who had broken their agreement with God. God was about to punish them for their sins. People thought they were secure even though they were sinners because the temple, the symbol of God's presence, was in their midst. Jeremiah wept and prophesied about Judah's idolatry. He warned the people of Judah of God's inevitable judgment against them. Jeremiah did see hope for the future (23:5) that the future savior who would form a 'new agreement' with His people (31:3). As we might expect, the New Testament points to Jesus Christ as the person who fulfills Jeremiah's expectation.

Christology

Jeremiah is one of the most Christ like personalities in the Old Testament. He showed great compassion for his people and wept for them. He suffered much but forgave them. Jesus alludes to several passages from Jeremiah in His teaching...this house...den of thieves in your eyes? (7:11; Matt.21: 13). My people have been lost sheep (50:6, Matt.10: 6) etc.

Pneumatology

A symbol of the Holy Spirit is fire (5:14). Apart from the normal work of inspiring the prophet and revealing God's message to him, the Holy Spirit is the one to carry out the promise of a new covenant that will put God's law in the minds of His people and write it on their hearts.

Out Line

1. Judgment against Judah and Jerusalem (1-25)
2. Jeremiah's life (26-29)
3. Book of comfort (30-33)
4. Jeremiah's life (34-35)
5. Judgment against foreign nations (46-51)

Application

Sin always must be punished but true repentance brings restoration. Our idolatry, which consists of such things as wealth, talent or position, is called by new names, but the sin is the same and the remedy is the same. God calls for obedience to His commands in a pure covenantal relationship. Sin requires repentance and restoration but obedience leads to blessing and joy.

LAMENTATION

The title, Lamentations refers to the cries and groans of the broken prophet as he looks upon the scattered bodies and shattered ruins of the smoldering city. The book of Lamentations provides a portrait of that most significant period in which the divine and human elements are depicted as they confronted one another. It was a period of intense suffering, a time of rebellion; it was a period of contrition, penitence and resolution. Secondly, this book provides a mirror for the subsequent generation. Thirdly, the book of Lamentations is a descriptive recital of tragedy.

Authorship and Date

The unnamed author was an eyewitness of the events surrounding the capture, defeat and destruction of the city. Strong evidence points to Jeremiah. This book was obviously written soon after the destruction and siege of Jerusalem around 586 B.C.

Purpose

By looking at the book, we can see the dual purpose of its writing. They are:

1) It was to put into words for posterity, the enormous sense of loss and pain the survivors felt and to admit their sin as the primary cause.

2) To focus on the love and mercy of God and pray for healing and restoration in their relationship with Him.

Theme

The judgment of God is swift and severe, but His mercy is available to those who repent and return to Him. In other words, theological theme of the book can be summarized as follows: God's angry disciplinary judgment of His people, while severe and deserved, was not final, even in the aftermath of judgment, Judah's loving compassionate and faithful God remained the source of the nation and future hope for restoration.

Christology

This book shows how weak people are under the law and how unable they are to serve God in their own strength. This drives them to Christ (Rom. 8: 3). Even in these poems, however, glimpses of Christ shine through. He is our hope (3:21, 24, 29). He is the manifestation of God's mercy and compassion (3:22, 23, 32). He is our redemption and vindication (3:58, 59).

Pneumatology

Divine grief over the sins of Israel (2:1-6) remind us that the Holy Spirit was, and is still often grieved by our behavior (Isa. 63:10). Repentance is also an indication of the work of the Holy Spirit

Out Line

This book is an honest diary of a broken man who identifies with the very nation he preached.

1. A Lament 1:1-4:22

   i)   Jerusalem weeps 1:1-22

   ii)   The Lord punishes 2:1-22

   iii)   Hope in affliction 3:1-66

   iv)   Confession of sin 4:1-22

2. Prayer 5:1-22

   i)   Look and see 1-10

   ii)   How terrible 11-18

   iii)   Bring us back 19-22

Application

i.   The best way to survive grief is to express it.

ii.   Privileges do not protect us either from responsibility or from discipline.

iii. God often allows suffering in our lives to discipline us (Heb. 12: 3-17). Through it we learn to obey Him and become stronger Christians. Discipline will direct us to God, drive us to prayer and bring us into submission.

iv. Sufferings come from both sides: God's side and Satan's side. Sufferings from God are restorative but, from Satan are destructive.

EZEKIEL

The book has been named after its author, Ezekiel (1:3, 24:24). The name Ezekiel means 'strengthened by God'. Ezekiel sees visions, prophecies, parables, signs and symbols to proclaim and dramatize the message of God to His exiled people.

Authorship and Date

Internally, the book gives evidence that Ezekiel wrote the book that bears his name. He wrote in the first person (1:1,8:1,20:1,24:1), which also indicates the unity of the book, not multiple authorship. Ezekiel probably wrote the book within the time period of the events likely 593-570 B.C.

Purpose

The primary purpose for the book of Ezekiel is to magnify God. About 70 times in the book, Ezekiel quotes the Lord "they will know that I am the Lord."

Message

Fundamentally, the theology or message of Ezekiel revolves around the bipolar themes of judgment and restoration. Judgment, was already a foregone conclusion, for he himself was living among the Jewish exiles in Babylonia and was reminded constantly that the state of affairs was a direct result of God's judgment on His wayward people. Restoration will take two forms. It will come to pass, in history, the beneficent policy of Cyrus the Persian, but that is only a foretaste, of complete renewal and reconstitution that must wail the eschaton. Spiritual renovation ended, resurrection life, will be part and parcel of that day of grace. Through her king, the Messiah of David, she will at last be a holy nation and kingdom of priest and fit in every way to administer, saying blessing to all the peoples of the earth.

Christology

Messiah is the part of his eschatological vision. The title 'Son of man' occurs 80 times in this book. Ezekiel is regarded as a type of Christ. (11:5; Luke 4:18,19). Divine shepherd in 34:11-16 is parallel to good shepherd in John 10:11-16. The root of Jesse (Isa. 11:1, 10; Rom. 15:12), serves to represent the future messiah, birds and trees represent Gentile nation to show Christ's universal reign.

Pneumatology

This book is called, as the acts of the Holy Spirit in Old Testament. There are numerous references to the Spirit of God in the book. Whether the prophetic revelation is presented symbolically in visions, signs, parabolic action or inhuman speech, Ezekiel claims for them the power and authority of the Holy Spirit.

Out Line

1. Call and commission of Ezekiel 1:1-3:27

2. Judgment follows sin 4:1-32: 32
   Against Israel 4:1-24:27
   Against the nations 25:1-32:32

3. Restoration follows judgment 33:1-48:35
   Consolation 33:1-39:29
   Renewed worship 40:1-48:35

Application

There is individual moral responsibility to meet. Though God is reluctant to discipline His people severally, He must. He is a righteous and jealous God, as much as He is merciful and forgiving. God will ultimately triumph in history.

DANIEL

Daniel was the first among the Jews to be taken into captivity by the Babylonians in 605 B.C. The book of Daniel is full of dreams and visions. Very detailed descriptions of future events are depicted and cryptically explained in this book. Daniel himself is very outstanding. He remains an example of uncompromising loyalty to God in the midst of a godless culture.

Authorship and Date

Daniel (God is Judge) wrote this book around 536B.C. He was the beloved prophet of God. He lived in Babylon throughout the entire 70 years of captivity. He was appointed as a trusted aid to King Nebuchadnezzar. God used him as His spokesman and prophet primarily to the king and the Gentile world.

Purpose

1. The main purpose of this book is to state the significant events during an era of gentile dominance.

2. Its purpose was to predict and briefly describe a Messianic kingdom, which will follow the period of Gentile supremacy.

Theme

The book of Daniel was the greatest prophetic declaration of sovereignty of God. It was no longer a theoretical matter but rather it had been manifested in the great events of history. First, the Lord brought Judah to His knees at the hands of Babylonians, chosen and used them as His instruments of judgment. Second, the Babylonians had been wrestled to the ground by the sovereign work of God in history.

The book of Daniel is a bridge that, like no other prophetic book, connects the two realms of Israel's history, the realm of tragic failure and the realm of incredible restoration. The chasm that the exile had created in history, through humiliation and despair, is spanned by Daniel, a bridge built of the basic stuff of prophetic belief and proclamation.

Christology

Christ is first seen as the 4th man standing with Shadrach, Meshach and Abed-Nego in the fiery furnace (3:25). The three remained faithful to God and now God stands faithful with them in the fire (3:27).

Another reference of Christ is found in Daniel's night vision (7:13). He describes, one like the Son of Man approached him, surrounded by clouds of heaven. Further vision of Christ is found in 10:5,6.

Pneumatology

The Holy Spirit never announces His presence in Daniel, but He is clearly at work. The ability of Daniel and the other Hebrews to interpret dreams was through the power of the Holy Spirit.

Out Line

1. The setting 1:1-21
2. The destinies of nations
   a. Gentiles: Powerless to oppose God 2:1-7:28
   b. Israel: Blessed for obeying God 8:1-12:12
3. Conclusion: A parting promise to Daniel 12:13

Application

1. Separation to God
2. Uncompromising Spirit
3. Courageous commitment
4. Absolute superiority of God
5. God is the God of the history

MINOR PROPHETS

The books from Hosea to Malachi are known as the minor prophetical books of the Old Testament. They are called so not because of their less value than the major prophetical books but because of their size of contents.

HOSEA

The book of Hosea is a one of the minor prophetic books playing major role. Hosea depicts the final decay of Israel just prior to her destruction and captivity by the Assyrians in 722 B.C. His personal life is the illustration for his message; his wife became a harlot, just like Israel had been to God. Hosea preaches sin, judgment because Israel failed to repent. The book of Hosea is full of pathos, as we read of a faithful and godly man who must endure the pain and embarrassment of a publicly unfaithful wife.

Authorship and Date

Hosea (salvation) was the last writing prophet to minister to the Northern kingdom of Israel's ten tribes before they fell to Assyria. Hosea is called *'the prophet of the broken heart'*. Hosea wrote this book during 725 B.C. shortly before the Assyrians' conquest.

Purpose

Hosea calls backslidden people to return to their God to avert the impending invasion of Assyria, God's promised judgment for their infidelity. God's love and mercy remain faithful and steadfast in the face of spiritual infidelity.

Message

Hosea's message is rooted in Israel's past in which Yahweh had expressed His over flowing love for His people by calling them out of Egypt (11:1). With tender nostalgia, He recalls His infant son's toddling days as He Himself taught him how to walk, taking him up in His arms (11:3), and under a different metaphor, leading him with 'bonds of love' (11:4). Judging from Hosea's imagery, we can be confident that He was a tender, a gentle father whose love knew no bounds. He saw Yahweh as that kind of Father to Israel. Motivated by love, Yahweh had called Israel out of Egypt (11:1, 12:13) spoken tenderly to and cared for him in the wilderness just as He would do again (2:14, 13:5) and secured him in the land of Canaan.

The primary imagery of the book is Hosea's marriage, which symbolized the marriage of Yahweh and Israel, Yahweh being the husband and Israel the wife (2:16). Prostitution was the symbol of idolatry. The aim that the Lord sought to achieve was the fidelity of Israel to Him alone. His emotional tie was one of love.

Christology

The New Testament writers draw upon Hosea for teaching about the life and ministry of Christ (Matt. 11:1). To Paul, Jesus fulfilled Hosea's promise that one would break the power of death and the grave and bring resurrection victory (13:14; I Cor. 15: 5).

Jesus even quotes Hosea to show that God desires not just empty words or heartless ritual, but genuine care and concern for people (6: 6, Matt. 9: 13).

Pneumatology

The book teaches two outstanding lessons concerning the Holy Spirit.

(1) It is important to depend upon the presence of the Spirit.

(2) Negative things happen when the Holy Spirit is missing from the life.

   The love of Hosea for his way-ward wife reminds us that the preeminent fruit of the Spirit is love (Gal. 5:22).

Out Line

1. Introduction 1:1

2. Hosea's marital experience 1:2-3:5

3. Hosea's message 4:1-14:9

   Yahweh's dispute with Israel 4:1-5:14

   A Liturgy of repentance of the realities of sin 5:15-6:10

   Images of judgment 6:11-7:16

   Religion and political improprieties 8:1-14

   Israel's harlotry of the prophet's behavior 9:1-9

   Images and infringements of covenant (9:10-11:12)

   History and harlotry 12:1-13:16

   Call to repentance and covenant renewal 14:1-9

Application

1. If the people around us do not see the love of God in us, they will not find it anywhere.

2. We cannot separate our witness and our ministries from our lives.

3. The only perfect example of love is found in God Himself.

JOEL

The book of Joel opens with an account of a recent locust plague that devastated Judah. Joel uses this national tragedy and a comparative basis for portraying the seriousness of the coming judgment of God.

Authorship and Date

Joel, son of Pethuel and prophet of God, is announced as the author of this book (1:1). Joel brings the Lord's Word to the nation of Judah. This book was written around 820 B.C. that is to say nearly 200 years before the Babylonian army devastated Judah in 586.

Theme

The prophet Joel brought a prophesy of judgment against the people of God, indeed the whole world. God is holy and in control of the whole world. So sinners will pay for their deeds. As with other prophets, Joel too was sent not only to preach judgment but also restoration of the relationship between God and His people.

Purpose

1. God wanted the Jews in Judah to know that He planned to judge their sin with great severity if they did not repent. He called them to return to Him with 'torn hearts' 2:13.

2. To establish a record for all nations for all time, that the day of the Lord will herald the end of human history.

Christology

Joel looked forward to a time when the Lord would bring judgment to the enemies of God and of Israel, when the nations would be called to give an account for their actions. He saw the day of great plenty flowing from the righteous reign of the Lord in Zion. Jesus is the one who will bring this age to a close, defeating His enemies, rewarding His church and setting up His final Kingdom of righteousness.

Pneumatology

Joel is remarkable in his references to the Holy Spirit. It is obviously the Holy Spirit who has inspired the prophet to see God's hand in all that is taking place and to be able to leap forward to the terrible day of the Lord.

Out Line

1.   Judah 1:1-2:11

     Sinful plague now 1:1-20
     The worst is yet to come 2:1-11

2.   Call to repentance 2:12-27

     Restoration is possible

3.   Gentile nations and Israel 2:28-3:21

     The era of the Spirit 2:28-29
     The day of the Lord 2:30-3:21

Application

Through the indwelling of the Holy Spirit, the church becomes the
Body of Christ in the world. The redemptive purposes of God are
therefore, extended and made available through every Spirit-filled
believer. Joel doesn't stop with the prediction of doomsdays; He
clearly announces the day of God's grace.

AMOS

Amos' name means 'burdened' or burden bearer. It is from a verbal
root that means '*load*' or '*carry a load*'. He certainly carried a weighty
Word from God. However, he was a layman, a shepherd, a dresser
of sycamore tree, until God tapped him for prophetic ministry (7:14).
With courage and conviction, he delivered God's message to Israel.
Amos' ministry may be dated sometime during the reign of Jeroboam
II in Israel. (787-746).

     Amos spoke for God to the Northern Kingdom of Israel while
the evil king was ruling. After getting victory in the battle, people
of God puffed up. They were living a life of complacency. Commerce
was flourishing, building was booming and the military was
enjoying the spoils of victory. Unfortunately, when they had tasted
power and wealth, they fell into sins of luxurious excess and the
moral and spiritual decay that accompanies them. In this critical
condition, God called Amos to preach about the coming judgment
for sin.

Authorship and Date

The writer was Amos, a native of the city of Tekoa just 6 miles South of Bethlehem in Judah. He probably wrote this book around 760 B.C.

Purpose

1. To warn the Northern Kingdom to return to the Lord or be judged.

2. To project the characteristics of God as a judge, if sin is continued and also merciful God willing to forgive and restore them if they will only repent.

Theme

The basic theme of Amos is the concept of God. God is the Creator and Sustainer of all He has made (4:13,5:8, 9:6). He rules the nations of the world (1:5, 2:9). Therefore, it is His right to judge (1:3-2:3) and He judges according to His own nature of righteousness. God is the righteous God. To reveal His righteousness, God has called out people and if they flout His standards and so deny His purpose, they can only expect His judgment (2:4, 4:12).

Christology

There are no direct references to Christ in Amos. There does seem to be an allusion however, to Amos 1:9, 10 in Jesus statement in Matt. 11:21, 22. Amos speaks of the judgment to come upon Tyre. Jesus says that if the mighty works performed in Chorazin and Bethsaida had been done in Tyre and Sidon, they would have repented long ago in sackcloth and ashes. An another concept from Amos is picked up by John in Revelation 10:7,11 is parallel to Amos 3:7.

Pneumatology

The work of the Holy Spirit is not mentioned in this book. The process of inspiring the prophets and revealing God's message is usually attributed by the other prophets to the Spirit (Isa. 48:16, Mic. 3:8). Amos doesn't happen to mention the Spirit in his work, but those activities ascribed to the Spirit by other prophets are present in Amos.

Out Line

1. The sins of Israel and her neighbors (1-2)
2. The condemnation of Israel (3-6)
3. The judgment of Israel (7:1-9:10)
4. The promise of restoration (9:11-15)

Application

1. One of the God's ordained foundations of society is justice between man and man. The gospel is not only a new relationship between man and God, but also a new relationship between man and man. If this right relationship is not evident in the life of the church, then the church becomes a shamble, heading for judgment.

2. Privilege entails or involves responsibility.

3. We are all responsible to live up to the measure of light granted to us.

4. Any form of worship, however scriptural it may be, is an insult to God if it is not accompanied by a life of practical righteousness. God first of all requires truth in the inner parts (Ps. 51:6), a truth that manifests itself in the relationships and conduct of every day. Only a worship based on this is acceptable to Him.

OBADIAH

The name Obadiah means '*Servant of Jehovah*'. He is one of the prophets in the Old Testament. Obadiah is the shortest book in the Old Testament (only 21 Verses). Obadiah is a little book, but it is an example of an atomic bomb in the Bible. It is small, but it has a potent message. Its message is primary, it is pertinent, it is practical and it is poignant. It is a message that can be geared into this day in which we are living.

Authorship and Date

Obadiah was the author of this brief message of doom. He

prophesied before the time of Joel, probably wrote sometime between 840-825 B.C.

Purpose

1) To announce judgment upon Edom.

2) To bring comfort and hope to God's people. Edom's hostile actions against Judah formed the basis for God's judgment. Judah's hope lay in the promises of restoration and exaltation.

Theme

Judgment is inevitable and ultimate even if it is not always immediately apparent. Those who despise Jehovah will by no means be exempted from the consequences of their unbelief.

Christology

Hebrew judges were saviors who foreshadow God's ultimate deliverer, Jesus Christ Himself - the Messiah. Through Jesus, God offers His Lordship and dominion to all mankind. Especially to the downtrodden and oppressed (Luke 4:16-21). The day of the Lord v. 15 and the Kingdom of God v.21 proclaimed by Obadiah anticipate the entry of Jesus Christ into the world.

Pnuematology

Even though there is no direct reference to the Holy Spirit, however He serves as Obadiah's source of inspiration, as the one who imparts the vision (v.1). He functions as the one who instigates the judgment of Edom etc., though God uses human agents to carry out, His justice behind it all is the working of His Spirit, prompting and punishing according to the plan of God.

Out Line

1) The title and introduction vs. 1

2) Edom vs. the Lord vs. 2-14

    i) The coming of destruction of Edom vs.1-9
    ii) Edom crimes against Judah vs. 10-14

3) Day of the Lord is near vs.15-21

i) Judgment of all nations vs.15-16
ii) Restoration of Judah vs. 17-21.

Application

The book calls into repentance of our pride to seek reconciliation in broken relationships and to model a lifestyle of forgiveness and acceptance (Matthew 5:21-26). Secondly, retribution is a reality, God is just. What we sow, we reap (v.15). Finally, in His sovereignty, God uses circumstances to accomplish His purposes, to purify and protect His people.

JONAH

The name of Jonah (in Hebrew Yonah) means dove. According to II King 14:25, he was the son of Amittai and his hometown was Gath – hepher. This village was located about 3 miles north east of Nazareth, Jesus' hometown.

Authorship and Date

Jonah is a historical character and the author of this book. The book was written towards the end of Jonah's career around 770 B.C.

Purpose

The main purpose of the book of Jonah is to show God's gracious dealing with the heathen Gentile city of Nineveh. God chose Jonah to be His channel of communication to its residents. The three main purposes of the book of Jonah are:

1) To teach God's people their responsibility to deliver the message of   salvation to all people: Jews and Gentile.

2) To demonstrate that God honors repentance for sin, whoever the person   (Jer. 18:7-10, Rom. 1:16).

3) To show to people of the Christian era that Christ death and resurrection, prefigured in Jonah's experience, were in the divine plan before Christ ever walked this earth.

Theme and Theology

1) This is the one book of the Old Testament, which sets forth the resurrection of Jesus Christ.

2)   The book teaches that salvation is not by works, but it is by
     faith, which leads to repentance (Jonah 2:9).

3)   God's purpose of grace cannot be concealed. Jonah refused to
     go to Nineveh but God knew how to get the message to Nineveh.

4)   God will not cast us aside for faithlessness. He may not use you
     but He   will not cast you aside.

5)   God is good and gracious (Jonah 4:2).

6)   God is the God of the Gentiles. The book of Jonah reveals that
     even in the Old Testament, God did not forget the Gentiles.
     God is in the business of saving sinners.

Christology

God's words to Jonah in 4:10,11 are paralleled by Jesus' words in
John 3:16. It is true that Christ has special relationship with members
of His body- the church but His love for the whole world was
dramatically demonstrated when He died on the cross for the sins
of all mankind. Universality of God's love (John 1:29). God loves
the world. His love for all men and women as taught to Jonah was
demonstrated ultimately in Jesus Christ (Matthew 24:31).

Pneumatology

When the Spirit-directed Jonah to go to Nineveh and prophesy
against the people there, the prophet refused to follow Lord's
guidance. The Spirit of God did not cease His work, but continued
to intervene in Jonah's life and induce him to do God's will.

Out Line

1)   Jonah's first commission 1:1-2:10
     Jonah flees 1:1-17
     Jonah prays 2:1-9
     Jonah is delivered 2:10

2)   Jonah's sacred commission 3:1-4:11
     Jonah preach 3:1-10
     Jonah complains 4:1-9
     God reproves 4:10-11

Application

1. Disobedience to God will create trouble in the life of a believer. Delayed obedience is disobedience.

2. Mission is the heartbeat of God.

3. Church is commissioned with special mission to the world (Matthew 28:18-20) without any discrimination. Gospel can bring the experience of mercy and forgiveness of God, which transforms the lives and cultures in peace and harmony.

MICAH

Micah was preaching the people and leaders of Judah at the same time when Isaiah and Hosea were executing their ministry in the Northern Kingdom of Israel.The residents of Judah were guilty of idolatry and political, social and spiritual decay. Micah especially addressed the issue of oppression of the poor by the rich. Micah was primarily a prophet to the Southern Kingdom of Judah.

Authorship

Micah is the author of this book. He lived in the country town of Moreshelh Gath, about 20 miles southern west of Jerusalem. He probably wrote the book around 730 B.C.

Purpose

The main purpose of writing this book was to announce the prophetic message to repent or judgment will come and comfort will eventually arrive. Micah also interjects a messianic message near the end, indicating that Israel's ultimate hope lies in the distant future.

Theme and Theology

God hates sin, but He loves the souls of sinners and He wants to save them. Judgment is called God's 'strange work'. It is strange because He doesn't like to judge. But since He is a holy and hates sin, any rebellion must be dealt with.He couldn't do otherwise. But He still loves the souls of sinners; He wants to save them and He will save them if they come to Him in faith.

Christology

Prophecies of Christ make Micah's book glow with hope and encouragement (1:3-5,2:12,13). The prophecy of 5:4,5 asserts the Messiah's shepherdhood (feed His flock), His anointing (in the strength of the Lord), His deity (in the majesty of the name of the Lord) and humanity (His God), His universal dominion etc.

Pneumatology

There is the mighty move of the Holy Spirit especially in the ministry of Micah. While other men were made bold by intoxicants to fabricate tales in the format of prophesy, the true power, might and justice behind Micah's message came from his anointing by the Spirit of the Lord (3:8).

Out Line

1) God of judgment 1:1-2:13

    i)   The people's corruption 1:1-2:11
    ii) God's promise of deliverance 2:12-13

2) God of hope 3:1-5:15

    i)   The leader condemned 3:1-12
    ii) The coming kingdom 4:1-5:15

3) God of pardon 6:1-7:20

    i)   The Lord's complaint 6:1-7:6
    ii) The Lord's forgiveness 7:7-20

Application

Micah has much to contribute to the knowledge of one's ongoing relationship with the Lord Jesus Christ. Relief from the foremost morals and religious sins of greed and idolatry in that ancient day can be had today by following Jesus in to the Kingdom of God. Micah's prophecy should make everyone stand in awe of the incomparable Yahweh who revealed Himself in the humanity of Jesus as the compassion of truth of God personified.

NAHUM

The name Nahum means comfort or consolation. In 722 B.C, the Assyrians invaded and destroyed the Northern Kingdom of Israel, and in 701 B.C they invaded Judah. At this juncture of history, Assyria was drunk with power and wealth. She would not acknowledge her sin or listen to God. Their fall was the inevitable consequences of pride and destruction. God commissioned Nahum to pronounce doom on Nineveh. Not many years later in 612 B.C. Nineveh was crushed and demolished by the Babylonians, Medes and Scythians, never to be rebuilt again. Justice is sure, though not always immediate.

Authorship and Date

The prophet Nahum wrote the book that bears his name (1:1). It was written during the years 650-620 B.C. This book was written to the people of Judah.

Purpose

There are mainly two purposes of this book:

i)   This book was written to pronounce judgment on the evil city of Nineveh.

ii)   And to offer hope and encouragement to Judah, God's people who have been oppressed by Nineveh.

Theme

The book of Nahum is filled with a variety of judgment speeches against Nineveh. While this book was a bad news for that city, it was a good news for Nahum's audience, the people of Judah who lived under the shadow of that superpower. God will judge the unrighteous and vindicate the righteous. When God makes a prediction about final judgment, it comes to pass.

Christology

Nahum's prophecy proclaims that God cannot countenance evil that sin must be cut off from the earth. At the crucifixion of Christ,

God drove the final nail into sin's coffin by sacrificing His own Son (Matt. 27:46, II Cor. 5:21). Nahum proclaims that God is good but His goodness was brought to its climax only in Christ (Rom. 5:6-11). God' goodness was enfleshed in Jesus, a living declaration of the good tidings of peace and love. The wicked lioness (2:11,12) has been defeated and replaced by the righteous lion of the tribe of Judah (Rev 5:5). God's vengeance against sin has been satisfied through the sacrifice of His Son.

Pneumatology

The Holy Spirit functions here as the Revealer, the one who reveals God's purpose to Nahum, the drama that unfolds before him and imparts the message from the Lord. He is commissioned to deliver. By the work of the Spirit, the Lord mustered His troops and led them in to victorious battle.

Out Line

1. The Lord's Majesty 1:1-2:2
    Nineveh's judge 1:1-8
    Nineveh's fall and Judah's protection 1:9-2:2

2. Nineveh's destruction 2:3-3:19
    The fall 2:3-13
    The causes 3:1-19

Application

i)   Seriousness of sin. Sin is the spiritual dangerous disease.

ii) Serious self-examination, which should lead us to wholehearted repentance.

iii) A life of wickedness eventually will lead to isolation, not only from other people, but also from God (3:19). The antidote for discouragement among believers is a revitalized vision of the person and power of God. True faith leaves judgment in the hands of God. The truth of God's judgment upon sin and the sinner should prompt believers to a renewed evangelistic mission.

HABAKKUK

Habakkuk was the final voice of God to Judah before she was destroyed and carried off to captivity by the Babylonians. Despite the powerful and continual ministry of the prophets, Judah had degenerated into an ungodly and idolatrous nation by the time Habakkuk addressed them (II Chr. 36:14-16). His message is dripping with passion (1:3)

Habakkuk was frustrated with the cold heartedness of his country men, but he was also upset that God hadn't done anything about it. Yet God responds to him by telling him that the Babylonians are about to became His agents of justice. God uses the wicked to achieve His purpose and the issue of ultimate justice.

Authorship and Date

Habakkuk himself wrote this book. Habakkuk prophesied and wrote sometimes during the reign of Josiah and perhaps Jeharakim (640-598).

Purpose

Through the passionate voice of Habakkuk, God assured the godly people of Judah who were having difficulty in understanding His divine ways. Finally, Habakkuk learns to wait on God and His perfect timing and he realizes that the people who are right must live by faith. (2:4)

Theme

Any nation that trusts in itself rather than God will fall. The book of Habakkuk is a conversation between God and the prophet about the evil prevailing in Judah. Habakkuk is confused about God's lack of response to the sin of Judah and His use of a wicked nation (Babylon) to judge Judah. God at last reveals to the prophet His plan to judge the evil doers (both in Judah and later in Babylon).

Christology

The terms used by Habakkuk in 3:13 join the idea of salvation with the Lord's anointed. The apostle Paul sees this statement 'the just shall live by faith' (2:4) of Habakkuk as the foundation stone of the Gospel of Christ (Rom. 1:16,17). Christ is the answer to human needs, including cleansing from sin, relationship with God and hope for the future.

Pneumatology

In Galatians, Paul links the most famous verse from this book with the reception of the promised Holy Spirit through faith (2:4, Gal. 3:11-14). The righteous person lives by his faith in all aspects of his life, including entering into the life of the Spirit.

Out Line

1. Habakkuk's complaints 1:2-17

   His first question 1:2-4
   God's answer 1:5-11
   His second question 1:12-17
   God's answer 2:1-20

2. Habakkuk's prayer 3:1-19

Application

When Habakkuk was troubled, he brought his concerns directly to God. After receiving God's answer, he responded with a prayer of faith. Habakkuk stands as a model for us. We don't have to be afraid to ask questions from God. The problem is not in God's ways, but is in our limited understanding of Him.

ZEPHANIAH

Zephaniah was a prophet to Judah during the reign of Josiah, last of the kingdom's righteous rulers. The sins, Zephaniah condemns in this book were the very sins over which the nation and king lamented.

Zephaniah prophesied judgments for Jerusalem that began to fall within a half a century. The same prophesies refer to judgment of end times, followed by restoration of the Jews who repented their rejection of the Messiah.

Authorship and Date

Zephaniah, a contemporary of Jeremiah wrote this book. It was written probably near the end of Zephaniah's ministry (640-621 B.C) when King Josiah's great reforms began.

Purpose

The main purpose of this book is to shake the people of Judah out of their complacency and urge them to return to God.

Theme

Zephaniah warned the people of Judah that if they refused to repent, the entire nation, including Jerusalem, would be lost. The people knew that God would eventually bless them, but Zephaniah made it clear that there would be judgment first, then blessing. This judgment would not be merely punishment for sin but also a process of purifying the people. Though we live in a fallen world surrounded by evil, we can hope for the perfect Kingdom of God to come. We can allow any punishment that touches us now to purify us from sin. This is what is the main theme of the book.

Christology

The meaning of Zephaniah's name (the Lord has hidden) conveys the ministry of Jesus Christ. The truth of the Passover in Egypt, where those hidden behind blood-marked doors were protected from the angel of the death is repeated in the promise of 2:3, where those meek on the earth, who have upheld God's justice, will be hidden on the day of Lord's anger. The rejoicing over a saved remnant (3:16,17) is connected with the work of Jesus, the Savior.

Pneumatology

A joyous work of the Holy Spirit is found in the promise that God will restore to the people, a pure language, that they may serve Him with one accord (3:9).

Out Line

1. The day of wrath 1:1-3:8
2. The day of hope 3:9-20

Application

1. To escape God's judgment we must listen to Him, accept His correction, trust Him and seek His guidance.

2. Don't let material comfort be a barrier to your commitment to God. Prosperity can produce an attitude of proud, self-sufficiency.

3. When people are purged of sin, there is great relief and hope. After refining process, there will be the moments of restoration and refreshment.

HAGGAI

Haggai was the first among the group of Jews who returned to Jerusalem from Babylon in 536B.C. People started the enormous task of rebuilding the temple, but soon opposition from outsiders discouraged them to the point of quitting altogether (Ezra 6:14a).

Once discouraged, the people become self-satisfied, neglecting the things of God in favors of personal pursuits. They were building nice homes for themselves, but God's dwelling place was in ruins. So, God raised up Haggai and Zechariah to stir them up, urging them to resume the rebuilding of God's temple. The people responded and in 516 B.C., they completed the task.

Authorship and Date

The author Haggai (festival of God) was probably a Babylonian born Jew. He and Zechariah were companions in the prophetic ministry. This book was written around 520 B.C., 16 years after the pilgrimage from Babylon to Jerusalem.

Purpose

The main purpose of this book was to call the people to complete the rebuilding of the temple and to warn them of their negligence and misplaced priorities.

Theme

Although Haggai is a short book, it is filled with challenge and promise, reminding us of God's claim on our lives and our priorities

Christology

Two references to Christ as the horn of Haggai are mainly high lighted. First in 2:6-9 and the second in 2:23. The book closes with a mention of Zerubbabel who is sign of a man chosen by God, from whose yielded nature of God causes to flow life, leadership and ministry. What he did in part, Jesus did in full as the servant of the Lord. Zerubbabel is also in the line of Messiah.

Pneumatology

Haggai 2:5 explains how the Holy Spirit of God is meant to interact with the spirit of the people in order to get the work accomplished.

1. The Holy Spirit is a vital part of God's covenant with His people.

2. The Holy Spirit is an abiding gift to the people of God.

3. The presence of the Holy Spirit removes fear from the hearts of God's people.

Application

1. It is easy to make other priorities more important than doing God's work. Get your priorities straight. Prioritize the things in life.

2. If God gives you a task, don't be afraid to get it started. His resources are infinite. God will help you to complete it by giving you encouragement from others along the way.

Out Line

1. The charge to resume building 1:1-11
2. The work is begun 1: 12-15
3. Encouragement to finish the work 2:1-23
4. Encouragement 2:1-9
5. Blessing 2:10-19
6. Zerubbabel honored 2:20-23

ZECHARIAH

Zechariah is the longest of the minor prophets. He preached a message of encouragement to the temple builders who had returned with him, under the leadership of Zerubbabel in 536 B.C. When God began to reveal His message to Haggai, which he had to proclaim, at that time, Zechariah was serving the Lord as a priest. But soon, the Lord called him to the ministry of prophet as well. While Haggai had both feet firmly planted in the present, Zechariah and his message gaze towards the future. Haggai prods the people to use their hands; Zechariah encourages them to open their hearts. Haggai was concerned about the physical dwelling place of God – the temple in Jerusalem; Zechariah's passion was for God's spiritual abode – the hearts of His people.

Authorship and Date

Zechariah (the Lord remembers) the grandson of Iddo, wrote this book sometime around 520B.C., after the first return to Jerusalem.

Purpose

1. To bring about spiritual revival among people.

2. To motivate and encourage the people to complete the temple.

3. To register officially same unmistakable prophecies about the coming Messiah (6:13,9:9,11:12-13,12:10,14:5,9)

Theme

For the present, there is pain for God's people, but a day will come when they will worship their God in His city, Jerusalem forever. The Lord remembers Zion.

Christology

Zechariah is sometimes referred to as the most messianic of all the old testament books. Chapters 9-14 are the most quoted section of the prophets in the passion of narratives of the gospels. Even in the Revelation, Zechariah is quoted more than any prophet except Ezekiel.

Jesus triumphal entry into Jerusalem is described in detail in 9:9, four hundreds years before the event (Matt. 21: 5; Mark 11:7-10).

Pneumatology

4:6 is the reference to the work of the Holy Spirit. Zerubbabel is comforted in the assurances that the rebuilding of the temple will not be by military might but by the ministry of the Spirit of God. Holy spirit will remove every obstacle that stands against the completion of God's temple.

Out Line

1. The way of salvation 1:1-6
2. Eight visions: Israel in history 1: 7-6:8
3. The harbinger of salvation; The Branch 6:9-15
4. Four messages; A testimony of the world 7:1- 8:23
5. The city of salvation: Jerusalem 9:1-14:21

Application

1. We must complete the task God has given us.

2. As we live in harmony, with God's purpose to restore what has lain desolate, we rest in the assurance that God's sovereignity governs the affairs of the earth.

MALACHI

When Malachi wrote this book, the Jews as a nation were back in Canaan and were living there for nearly one hundred years. They were discouraged and disappointed. The promise of their grandparents seemed to be nothing more than an old story or a legend. Their faith and worship was slowly eroding; it was beginning to surface in their day-to-day relationships as well. God was willing to dialogue with His people, but tragically, their hearts are hardened by sin. In this context, Malachi came as a last voice from God before 400 years of silence.

Authorship and Date

Malachi, a contemporary of the leader Nehemiah, wrote this book. He probably wrote this book around 433B.C, the time of Nehemiah's visit to Babylon recorded in Nehemiah 13:6.

Purpose

1. To confront the people of their sins.

2. To call them back to God.

3. To arouse the sense of balancing their accountability to the Law of Moses with their unchanging love of God.

Theme

The Lord doesn't change. That means both His mercy and His holiness are operative. God loves His people even when they neglect or disobey Him. He has great blessings to bestow on those who are faithful to Him. His love never ends. God's love for His faithful people is demonstrated by the Messiah's coming. He will lead them to the realization of all their fondest hopes. It will be the day of comfort and healing for a faithful few and a judgment for those who reject Him.

Christology

There is clear prophetic utterances regarding the sudden appearance of Christ, the Messenger of the new covenant (3:1). No one can in his own strength but for those who fear the Lord, stand when He appears. He is the Son of Righteousness, Jesus (He shall arise with healing in His wings, that is, in victorious triumph (4:2)).

Pneumatology

The working of the Holy Spirit in Malachi is evident in his own personal life and prophetic ministry. The Holy Spirit granted to him the privilege of bringing the line of faithful, dedicated writing prophets to a close, by allowing him to proclaim with clarity and fervency, his telescopic vision of Christ's coming.

Out Line

1. Declaration of God's love 1:1-5

2. Disapproval of unfaithful priest 1:6-2:9

3. Denunciation of backslidden people 2:10,4:3

4. Declaration of final warning 4:4-6

The book of Malachi forms a bridge between the Old Testament and the New Testament.

Application

God deserves our very best honor, respect and faithfulness. But sin hardens our hearts to our true condition. We should not let pride keep us from giving God our devotion, money, marriage and family.

CHAPTER – 3

ADVENTURE THRU'
THE NEW TESTAMENT

THE GOSPELS AND THE HISTORY

The Old Testament constitutes the preparation for Christ and contains prophecies of His divine person and redemptive work. The New Testament is the account of the realization of these predictions in the appearance of the Redeemer.

As far as the four gospels are concerned, they are neither histories of the life of Christ nor biographies. They are rather the portraits of the Person and work of the long promised Messiah, Israel's King and the world's Savior. As portraits, they present four different poses of one unique personality. Matthew by the Holy Spirit presents Christ as King, Mark as Servant, Luke as Man and John as God.

In their fourfold portraiture of Christ's Person as King, Servant, Man and God, the gospels center in Messiah's threefold ministry of Prophet, Priest and King. As prophet, fulfilling Moses great prediction (Deu.18: 15-19). He was the prophet par excellence by virtue of the uniqueness of His Person. He not merely spoke for God as other prophets who preceeded Him, but spoke through Him as Son (Heb.1:1-2). In contrast to the Old Testament prophet who was a voice for God, the Son, being God, was the voice of God Himself. As a Priest, Christ became both the sacrifice and the sacrificer as He died on the cross to save sinners (Heb. 9: 14) and through His resurrection, lives eternally to make intercession for them (Heb. 7:25). As Israel's King, He was rejected at first advent, but will reign in that office at His second advent, fulfilling the Davidic Covenant (II Sam. 7: 8-16, Luke 1:30-33, Acts 2:29-36, 15:14-17).

The gospels are designedly incomplete as a story, but marvelously complete and purposeful as a divine revelation of the Son of God our savior ! And this is faith's need. It is also unbelief's stumbling block.

THE SYNOPTIC GOSPELS

Matthew, Mark and Luke are usually known as the Synoptic Gospels. "Synoptic" comes from two Greek words, which mean '*to see together*', and literally means '*able to be seen together*'. These three gospels give an account of the same events in Jesus' life. There are additions and omissions in each of them, but broadly speaking their material is the same and their arrangement is also the same. There is the closest possible relationship between them. If we, for example, compare the story of the feeding of the 5000 (Matt. 14: 12-21, Mark 6: 30-44, Luke 9:10-17) we find exactly the same words. Another example is the story of the healing of the man who was sick with palsy (Matt. 9:1-8, Mark 2:1-12,Luke 5:17-26) These three accounts are so similar that even a little parenthesis 'he then said to the paralytic'- occurs in all three, as a parenthesis in exactly the same place. The correspondence between the three gospels is so close that we are bound to come to the conclusion that either all three are drawing their material from a common source, or that two of them must be based on the third.

THE EARLIEST GOSPELS

When we examine the matter more closely, we see that there is every reason for believing that Mark must have been the first of the gospels to be written and that the other two, Matthew and Luke are using Mark as a basis. Mark has 661verses: Matthew has 1068 verse: Luke has 1149 verses. Matthew reproduces no fewer than 606 of Mark's verses, and Luke reproduces 320 of the 55 verses of Mark which Matthew does not reproduce, Luke reproduces 31; so there are only 24 verses in the whole of Mark which are not reproduced anywhere in Matthew or Luke.

It is not only the substance of the verses, which is reproduced; the very words are reproduced. Matthew uses 51% of Mark's words;

and Luke uses 53%. Mark seems to be the summary of Matthew and Luke.

GOSPEL OF MATTHEW

Matthew is the Gospel, which was written for the Jews. It was written by a Jew in order to convince Jews. This gospel has a especially strong apocalyptic interest i.e., all that Jesus said about His own second coming, about the end of the world, and judgment. Matthew's dominating idea is that of Jesus as King. Jesus walks through his pages as if in the purple and gold of royalty, and Matthew is especially interested in the church; church after Peter's confession at Caesarea Philippi (Matt. 16:13-23); church as the great organization and institution and the dominant factor in the life of the Christian.

Authorship and Date

The author of this gospel is Matthew, a Jewish tax collector who became a disciple of Jesus. Tax collectors were despised by the Jews because they helped to penetrate the cruel oppression of Israel through the enforcement of unjust and often illegal taxation. Most Jews would have considered Matthew a 'traitor'. This makes Jesus' selection of him as a disciple all the more significant. Matthew's Gospel was probably composed in the late 50's or 60's A.D. We can guess this because the Jewish temple was destroyed by Roman commander, Titus in A.D.70 and Matthew certainly would have mentioned it is in his gospel if it had recently occurred. But there is no trace of it. That is a strong reason for saying that this gospel was written before the destruction of the Jerusalem temple.

Matthew especially had Jews in mind when he wrote his account of Jesus, the Messiah, but he also wrote for non-Jews as well. The world in which Matthew lived was very metropolitan. The Jewish nature of the gospel suggests that it was written in Palestine.

Purpose

One of the greatest purpose is to demonstrate that all the prophecies of the Old Testament are fulfilled in Jesus, and that therefore, He must be the Messiah. He does this primarily by showing how Jesus in His life and ministry fulfilled the Old Testament Scriptures. To accomplish his purpose, Matthew also emphasizes Jesus' Davidic lineage.

Theme

The essential key to Matthew's theology is that, in Jesus all God's purposes have come to fulfillment. The Old Testament points forward to Him; its law is fulfilled in His teaching, He is the true Israel through whom God's plans for His people now go forward, the future no less than the present is to be understood as the working out of the ministry of Jesus. History revolves around Him, in that His coming is the turning point at which the age of preparation gives way to the age of fulfillment. In His coming, a new age has dawned, nothing will ever be quite the same again.

Christology

Matthew's view of Jesus is the one who fulfills the whole fabric of scriptural revelation of the Old Testament. In the gospel, Jesus often refers to Himself as the Son of Man; a veiled reference to His Messiahship (Dan. 7:13,14). Matthew presents Jesus as Lord and Teacher of the church, the new community, which is called to live out the new ethic of the Kingdom of Heaven. Jesus declared 'the church as His select instrument for fulfilling the purposes of God on earth (16:18,18:15-20). Matthew's Gospel may have served as a *teaching manual* for the early church, including the amazing world oriented great commission (28:12-20) with its guarantee of Jesus' living presence.

Pneumatology

It was by the power of the Spirit that Jesus was conceived in Mary's womb (1:18,20). Before Jesus began His public ministry, He was filled with the Spirit of God (3:16) and followed the Spirit's leading into the wilderness to be tempted by the devil as further preparation for His Messianic role (4:1). The power of the Holy Spirit enabled Jesus to heal (12:15-21) and to cast out demons (12:28).

Out Line

1. The birth and early years of Jesus 1-2
2. The beginning of Jesus' ministry 3:1-4:11
3. Galilean ministry of Jesus 4:12-14:12
4. Jesus withdrawals from Galilee 14:13-17:20
5. Jesus last ministry in Galilee 17:22-18:35
6. Jesus ministry in Judæa and Perea 19-20
7. Passion week 21-27
8. The resurrection 28

Application

Christian disciples must learn to live within the tension of two ages, the present age of fulfillment in the Person of Jesus and the age to come i.e., the consummation of all things. In the interim, Christians are called to be humble, patient, genuine, faithful, watchful and responsible, assured of the presence of the risen Jesus as they are expectant of His return when faith will give way to sight.

The Kingdom of God (in Matthew Kingdom of Heaven) is a spiritual Kingdom of heavenly character, nature and order. It refers specially to where the rule and the reign of God is made effective by submission to the spiritual principles of the King.

MARK

The Gospel of Mark is a succinct, unadorned yet vivid account of the ministry, suffering, death and resurrection of Jesus. Mark presents the narrative in an appealing way, for he tells the good news about Jesus Christ so simply that a child can understand it. Nevertheless like a pool of pure water, it is far deeper than it looks. Therefore one ought to approach the study of this book humbly and with due recognition of the need for wisdom from the Almighty God and enlightenment from the Holy Spirit.

Authorship and Date

Though strictly speaking Mark's Gospel is anonymous, the early tradition of the church identifies the author with Mark, who was closely associated with the apostle Peter and from whom he received the tradition of the things said and done by our Lord. This tradition did not come to Mark as a finished, sequential account of the life of Jesus but in the form of the preaching of Peter, preaching that had been directed to the needs of the early Christian community. It is this material arranged and shaped by Mark, that forms the nucleus of this gospel.

It is not possible to date Mark's Gospel with precision. Although we cannot be certain of it, the best estimate dating of the gospel is the last half of the decade A.D 60-70. This date embraces the period immediately following the great fire of A.D 64 when intense persecution began to be directed against Christians in Rome. The Gospel of Mark was written to meet this crisis in the Roman church.

The way Mark prepares his Christian readers for suffering is by placing before them the passion experience of Jesus. The way of discipleship for Christians is the same way -way of the cross: faithfulness and obedience.

Purpose

The meaning of Mark's Gospel can be best understood as we bear in mind the purpose for which it was written. Mark's supreme object (purpose) was to show the Gentile world the active love of God in Jesus Christ, serving needy men, seeking after sinners and saving all who trusted Him. Another purpose of this gospel is to encourage and strengthen the persecuted church at Rome.

Theme

There was a growing apprehension among the early Christians concerning the martyrdom of the saints. They were constantly asking, why do God's good servants have to die such cruel deaths? The widely heralded executions of Paul and Peter were quite fresh in the minds of the Christians of that day. Besides, many of them had been stunned by the ruthless slaughter of their own relatives and friends, for no other reason but that they were Christians. In addition to all of this, Jesus Himself, the Son of God, had suffered death upon a cross. How could these things be? The early Christians needed a strong word of encouragement and explanation.

Jesus died, Mark declared because of the hatred and antipathy of the religious leaders of His day. Jesus would not compromise the truth nor stand aside from His divinely appointed mission, even though it should mean His death upon a cross. Christians of every generation must stand firm and unafraid in the face of the most brutal persecution. The way of the Christians is the way of the cross - the way of self-renunciation and self sacrifice (8:31,9:31,10:32-34).

Jesus died because He chose to die. For that very purpose, He came to earth (10:45). Christ died for the sins of the world. The death of Jesus was not simply a tragedy. It was all in accordance with the divine purpose to overcome the evil one and effect redemption for sin.

The sufferings of saints also have a place in the plan and the purpose of God, though to a far less degree. In truth, the blood of the martyrs would become the seed of the church. This is the main theme of the Gospel of Mark.

Christology

This book is not a biography, but a concise history of redemption accomplished through the atoning work of Christ. Mark substantiates the Messianic claims of Jesus by emphasizing His authority as a teacher (1:22) and His authority over Satan and unclean spirits (1:27,3:19-30), sin (2: 1-12), the sabbath (2:27), nature (4:35), disease (5:21-34), death (5:35-43), legalistic traditions (7:1-13,14-20) and the temple (11:15-18).

Pneumatology

Of particular encouragement to Christians facing the hostility of unjust authorities is the Lord's assurance that the Holy Spirit will speak through them when they testify of Christ (13:11). In addition to explicit references to the Holy Spirit, Mark employs words associated with the gift of the Spirit, such as power, authority, prophet, healing, laying on of hands, Messiah and Kingdom.

Out Line

1.   The beginning of Jesus' ministry 1:1-13

2. Jesus' ministry in Galilee 1:14,6:29
3. Withdrawals from Galilee 6:30,9:32
4. Final ministry in Galilee 9:33-50
5. Jesus' ministry in Judæa and Perea 10
6. The passion of Jesus 11-15
7. The resurrection of Jesus 16

Application

Mark's Gospel teaches that the life of discipleship means following Jesus even if it is a path of rejection that He encountered. It assures Christian workers of all generations that the same attesting miracles that accredited the ministries of the apostles will continue as characteristic features of God's people under the New Covenant (16:17,18). He that humbles himself under the hands of God shall be exalted in due time (I Peter 5:6).

GOSPEL OF LUKE

At the heart of Luke's Gospel is the picture of a shepherd rejoicing over the recovery of a lost sheep, a woman rejoicing over the recovery of a lost coin, a father rejoicing over the recovery of the one son and pleading with another son to join the family in joyous reunion. God is like that. In brief, that is what the Gospel of Luke is all about. It is about God's concern for all people, His joy over each one recovered – Jew, Samaritan or Gentile. It is about God's concern with all the needs of all people : that the blind see, the deaf hear, the lame walk, the lepers are cleansed, those in bondage are freed and that sinners are forgiven.

Authorship and Date

Church tradition names Luke, the non-Jewish physician, as the author of this account of the good news of Jesus. Theophilus, a highly respected individual, is especially named as the recipient of this book in 1:3. However, Luke is clearly writing to both Jewish and non-Jewish Christians. This book was most likely written in Rome.

The book of Acts, which continues Luke's accounts in this book, ends with Paul's house arrest in Rome. So the most likely date when Luke wrote his gospel was in AD 62-63.

Purpose

The gospel was written out of faith unto faith in order to hold up Jesus, as Lord and Redeemer. Luke wrote this gospel with the object of convincing, converting, saving and spiritually edifying his fellow men.

The main purpose of Luke was to present Jesus as no mere Jewish Messiah, but a world - Savior. This gospel was written to strengthen the faith of all believers and to answer the attacks of unbelievers. Luke wanted to show that the place of the Gentile Christians in God's Kingdom is based on the teaching of Jesus.

Special features

1. Universal recognition of Gentiles as well as Jews in God's plan.

2. Emphasis on prayer, especially Jesus praying before important occasions (3:21).

3. Joy at the announcement of the gospel (1:14).

4. Special concern for the role of women.

5. Special interest in the poor and lowly.

6. His concern for sinners (Jesus was the friend of those who are deep in sin.)

7. Stress on the family circle.

8. Emphasis upon the Holy spirit (4:1)

Theme and Theology

Jesus, the Son of Man loves mankind and offers God's salvation from their sins (19:10) A running theme in Luke's Gospel is Jesus' compassion for Gentiles, Samaritans, women, children, tax collectors, sinners and others, often regarded as outcasts in Israel. The main theme and theology of Luke can be described as follows:

1. Universality of Salvation

God's love is for all people and His salvation reaches far and wide. Luke tells us that the message of angel concerning people in general, not specially Israel (2:14). He takes the genealogy of Jesus right back to Adam (3:38), the progenitor of mankind and doesn't stop at Abraham, the father of the Jewish nation. He tells us about Samaritans (9:5-54). He refers to Gentiles in the song of Simeon (2:32). Through all these, it is clear that Luke has a deep interest in God's concern for all people.

2. The Plan of God

Luke saw God, as working out a great plan in human affairs. He was clear that people do not defeat God. The death of Jesus was not the result of Jesus' defeat or failure rather it was the redemptive plan of God. Luke was clear that, God is not some remote Olympian, aloof from the human race and careless about its fate. Rather He is interested in our salvation and constantly at work in human affairs to bring to pass His redemptive purpose.

Christology

(1) Jesus is the prophet whose role becomes equated with servant and Messiah (4:24,7:16).

(2) Jesus is the ideal man, the perfect Savior of imperfect human kind.

(3) Jesus is the promised Messiah in the Old Testament (9:31, 51).

(4) Jesus is the exalted Lord. Luke refers to Jesus as Lord 18 times in his gospel.

(5) Jesus is the friend to the lowly and outcastes. He is consistently gracious to society's rejected ones, publicly acknowledged sinners, Samaritans, Gentiles and the poor. Jesus' ministry is of kindness and compassion. Jesus is the Savior of the whole world.

Pneumatology

There are many references to the Holy Spirit in Luke stressing His activity both in the life of Jesus and in the continuing ministry of the church.

(1) The Holy Spirit's action is seen in the lives of various faithful people (1:35,41,67,2:25-27).

(2) The Holy Spirit enabled Jesus to fulfill His ministry as the Spirit anointed Messiah.

(3) The Holy Spirit, through petitionery prayer, effects the Messianic ministry.

(4) The Holy Spirit spreads joy, both to Jesus and the new community of faith (24:52,53).

Out Line

1. Preface 1:1-4
2. The infancy narratives 1:5-2:52
3. The ministry of John the Baptist 3:1-20
4. The beginning of Jerusalem 3:21-4:13
5. Jesus in Galilee 4: 14-19:50
6. From Galilee to Jerusalem 9:51-19:44
7. Jesus is Jerusalem 19:45-21:38
8. The crucifixion 22:1-23:56
9. The resurrection 24:1-53

Application

Salvation is for people of caste, colour and sex. It is not only for freemen, but also for slaves and all others rejected by society the lowly, poor, the helplessly weak, the crucified thief, the outcast sinner, and the despised tax collector. He is with us in us and around us. He lifts us up from the nobody of the society to somebody for God's Kingdom.

GOSPEL OF JOHN

God's glory had dwelt in the tabernacle (Exo. 40:34) and in the temple (I Kings 8:10-11) but that glory had departed from disobedient Israel (Eze. 9:3,10:4,.18,.11:22-23). Then a marvellous thing happened. The glory of God came to His people again in the

Person of His Son, Jesus Christ. The gospel writers have given the glimpses of the earthly life of Jesus Christ. Matthew wrote with his fellow Jews in mind and emphasized that Jesus of Nazareth had fulfilled the Old Testament prophecies. Mark wrote for the busy Romans whereas Matthew emphasized on the King. Mark presented the Servant, ministering to needy people. Luke wrote his gospel for the Greeks and introduced them to the sympathetic Son of Man.

But John, the beloved disciple, wrote a book for both Jews and Gentiles, presenting Jesus as the Son of God. We know that John had Gentiles as well as Jews in mind. His emphasis on the Jews was that Jesus not only fulfilled the Old Testament prophecies, but He also fulfilled the types. Jesus is the Lamb of God (1:29) and the ladder from heaven to earth (1:51, Gen. 28). He is the new temple (John 2:19-21) and He gives a new birth (3:4ff). He is the serpent lifted up (3:14) and the Bread of God that came down from heaven (6:35ff).

Whereas the first 3 gospels described events from the life of Christ, John emphasized the meaning of these events. For example, all four gospels record the feeding of the 5,000 but only John records Jesus' sermon on 'the Bread of life', which followed that miracle when He interpreted it for the people.

Authorship and Date

Although he is not identified by name, but simply 'as the follower Jesus loved' (13:23), John the apostle is the most likely author of this book. He is the only major apostle not named, and he clearly was an eyewitness to many of the major events of Jesus' ministry.

John used some abstract concept in his book (e.g. the Word, Logos) which makes us believe that the book was written for Greeks, however, the author had an evangelistic purpose (20: 31) and the book speaks to both Jews and non- Jews. This book was written late in the John's life, Ephesus would be the most likely place of writing. Latest evidence, including the Dead Sea Scrolls, indicate John likely wrote this book between A.D. 50 and 70.

Purpose

John's purpose was to produce faith in people that Jesus is the God-man (incarnation) anointed to be the Savior of the world. It presents Jesus' deity clearly and teaches more about the Holy Spirit than the other three accounts of the good news.

Theme and Theology

The overall themes and message of the gospel is found in 20:31; "Jesus Christ, the Son of God." The book therefore centers on the Person and the work of Christ. Three predominant words: sign, believe and life receive constant emphasis throughout the gospel to enforce the theme of salvation in Him. Summing up, the gospel focuses on:

i)   Jesus as the Word, the Messiah and the Son of God.
ii) Jesus brings the gift of salvation to all mankind.
iii) It is the person who either accepts or rejects the free offer of everlasting life.

The Seven Signs in the Gospel and their Significance:

-   Turning the water into wine (Jn. 2:1-12) shows that Jesus is the source of life.

-   Healing a noble man's son (Jn. 4:46ff) shows that Jesus is the master over distance.

-   Healing a lame at Bethesda (Jn. 5:1ff) shows that Jesus is the master over time.

-   Feeding 5,000 with only two loaves of bread and five pieces of fish (Jn. 6:1ff) shows that Jesus is the bread of life.

-   Walking on the water, stilling a storm (Jn. 6:15ff) clearly shows that Jesus is the master over nature.

-   Healing a blind (Jn. 9:1ff) which shows that Jesus is the light of the world.

-   Raising Lazarus who was dead for four days (Jn. 11:17ff), that shows that Jesus has the power over the doom and death.

The 'I Am' Statement

Twenty three times, we find our Lord's meaningful I AM (*ego eimi*) in the Greek text of this gospel. In several of these, He joins His 'I AM' with seven tremendous metaphors, which are expressive of these saving relationships towards the world.

- I am the bread of life (Jn. 6:35,41,48 and 51)
- I am the light of the world (Jn.8: 12)
- I am the door of the sheep (Jn. 10:7,9)
- I am the good shepherd (Jn. 10:11,14)
- I am the resurrection and the life (Jn.11: 25)
- I am the way, the truth and the life (Jn. 14:6)
- I am the true vine (Jn. 15 :1,5)

* Eternal life is only available through Jesus Christ, the only Son of God.

Pneumatology

John's Gospel is unique in the designation of the Holy Spirit as Comforter or Helper (14:16). In regard to the world outside of Christ, He works as the agent who convicts of sins, righteousness and judgment (16:8ff). Holy Spirit's mission is to glorify Jesus and to declare Christ's teaching to the disciples (16:14). The Holy Spirit leads believers into an understanding of the meanings, implications, and imperatives of the gospel and enables them to do greater works than those done by Jesus (14:12). He is our contemporary for all times and ages.

Out Line

1. The incarnation of the Son of God (1:1-18)
2. The presentation of the Son of God (1:19-4:54)
3. The opposition to the Son of God (5:1-12:50)
4. The preparation of the disciples by the Son of God (13:1-17:26)
5. The execution of the Son of God (18:1-19:16)
6. The resurrection of the Son of God (19:38-21:23)
7. Conclusion (21:24-25)

Application

A positive response of faith in Jesus... the Christ, the Son of God results in life in His name. In 10:10, John makes it clear that life is not an independent quality unrelated to God or to Christ. The knowledge of the only true God and Jesus Christ (Jn.17: 3), which implies fellowship as well as intellectual understanding, is the key to the meaning of eternal life. Faith brings life; unbelief brings death.

THE BOOK OF ACTS OF THE APOSTLES

The book of Acts provides a bridge for the writings of the New Testament. As a second volume to Luke's Gospel, it joins what Jesus began to do and to teach (1:1) as told in the gospel with what he continued to do and teach through the apostle's preaching and the establishment of the church. Geographically, its story spans the land between Jerusalem, where the church began and Rome, the political center of the empire. Historically, it recounts the first 30 years of the church. It is also a bridge that lies between the church in its beginning and succeeding age. This book teaches us about the principles that ought to govern the church of any age.

Authorship and Date

The author of this book was:

(1) Luke, the companion of Paul

In the description of the happenings in Acts, certain passages make use of the pronoun 'we'. At these points, the author includes himself as a companion of Paul in his travel (16:10-17,20:5-21:18,27:1-28:16).

(2) Luke, the physician

Although, it cannot be proved that the author of Acts was a physician simply from his vocabulary, the words he uses and the traits and education reflected in his writings fit well in his role as a physician (28:6).

Since no reference is made to events after AD 63, this is the probable date of it's writing. This book was written for both Jews

and non-Jews of the last third of the first century. It was written at
Rome.

Purpose

The main purpose of the Acts of the Apostles was to present a
history of church and their spread. Secondly, to give a defense made
to both Jews and Gentiles (4:8-12 and 25:8-11).Thirdly, to provide
a guide for church planting and the mission of the church until the
second coming of Christ. Finally, it was to depict the triumph of
Christianity even in the face of bitter persecution.

Theme and Theology

Like the book of Luke, Acts is primarily about salvation: God's
purpose to bring salvation in all of its fullness to all people. The
primary force in the spread of the good news is the Holy Spirit. The
Spirit empowers and directs those who are involved
in the mission.

The vision for the mission is clear: from Jerusalem to Judæa to
Samaria and to every part of the world (Acts 1:8). God's grace has
gone out from Jerusalem to the rest of the world and God's people
must do the same. Every boundary must be crossed as people are
challenged with the good news of salvation.

Salvation in Acts has both personal and social implications.
Above all else, salvation means membership in the new community
of those who serve the will of God. Baptism[14] and the gift of the
Holy Spirit are both related to membership in this growing family
of believers. Salvation in Acts is also presented as the forgiveness
of sins; forgiveness means both restored relationship with God and
also admission of the unity of the church, as though its members
shared life together as a family.

---

[14] Baptism is one of the most significant and important religious sacraments
of Christianity. The word baptism comes from the Greek word meaning 'to
dip in or under water'. It is a total dipping (immersion) under the water. This
shows that Christians are united with Christ in His death, burial and
resurrection (Rom. 6 : 3,4). Through this union with Christ, their sins are
forgiven and washed away.

Christians should not necessarily expect trouble from authorities; instead, Christians are encouraged to maintain complete allegiance to God even when human authorities oppose them.

Christology

The book of Acts records several examples of the early Apostolic proclamation of the Gospel of Jesus Christ. Jesus is presented as a historical figure - a man empowered to perform signs and wonders (2:22,10:38). His death, resurrection, His exaltation has been emphasized in this book. From that place of supreme honor and executive power, Jesus had poured out the promised Holy Spirit (2:33), who bears witness to Him (5:32) and empowers believers (1:8). Jesus has been ordained by God to be judge of the living and the dead (10:42) and will return at the end of the age (1:11).

Pneumatology

The book of Acts is the story of the disciples receiving what Jesus did. The power of the Spirit in Jesus' life, authorized Him to preach, heal and set the captives free. The same Spirit's power in Acts 2 gave the same authority to the disciples. Jesus is the prototype of the Spirit-filled, Spirit empowered life (10:38).

Characterstics of Acts

1.   Accurate historical detail

Every page of Acts abounds with sharp, precise details, to the delight of the historian.

2.   Literary excellence

Paul uses words in literary style that fits the cultural settings of the events he was recording.

3.   Dramatic description

Luke's skillful use of speeches contribute to the drama of his narrative. They are well placed and well balanced in the book.

4.   Objective account

Paul demonstrates the objectivity of his account by recording the failures as well as the successes, the bad as well as the good, in the early church.

Out Line

The Beginning of the Christian Church

1. Jerusalem

   The church is born 1:1-2:47
   The church grows through testing 3:1-8:1

2. Judæa and Samaria

   The church is scattered 8:1b-9: 31
   The church embraces the Gentiles 9:32-12:25

3. Every part of the world

   The church extends overseas 13:1-21:17
   The church's leader on trial 21:18-28:31

Application

Acts is about ordinary people doing extraordinary things. Signs and wonders followed those who believed (Mark 16:17-18). Moreover, it is a record of practicing Christianity under the power of the Holy Spirit. Early Christians fasted and prayed fervently (2:42,6:4) and their faith released the miracle working power of God (3:16). Today it can happen if we commit ourselves completely and trust upon Him alone. He is on the move by His Holy Spirit. Only by the power of the Holy Spirit can the great commission be fulfilled (Zech. 4 : 6).

THE LETTERS

The letters from Romans to Jude are known as the letters.

DOCTRINAL LETTERS

These letters provide the doctrinal themes such as soteriology, eschatology and so on. The letters from Romans to 2 Corinthians are called the doctrinal letters.

ROMANS

The letter of Romans has been called the heart of the New Testament. By commenting about this book, Martin Luther, the father of Reformation once said, "This epistle is the chief part of the New Testament and the very purest gospel, which indeed deserves that a Christian not only know it word for word by heart, but deal with it daily as, daily bread of the soul. For it can never be read or considered too much or too well, and the more it is handled the more delightful it becomes, and the better it tastes."

Authorship and Date

The letter itself says that it was written by Paul, a servant of Christ Jesus, called to be an apostle and set apart for the Gospel of God (1:1)

Romans was apparently written between A.D. 54 and 58. Evidence indicates that Felix became the procurator of Judæa in AD 59, at the time when Paul was in custody in Caesarea (Acts 23:33-27:2). Allowing time for the journey from Corinth to Jerusalem and Paul's subsequent activity before his appearance before Festus, a date somewhere around AD 56 is most likely for the composition of Romans. When Paul wrote this letter, he was probably at Corinth (Acts 20:2-3) on his 3rd missionary journey.

Purpose

1. He wrote this letter to prepare the way for his coming visit to Rome and his proposed mission to Spain (1:10-15,15:22-29).

2. He wrote to present the basic system of salvation (by faith) to a church that had not received the teaching of an apostle before.

3. He sought to explain the relationship between Jews and Gentiles, in God's overall plan of redemption. The Jewish Christians were being rejected by larger group of Gentile in the church (14:1ff) because the Jewish believers still felt constrained to observe dietary laws and sacred days (14:2-6).

Theme and Theology

Paul's primary theme in Romans is the basic gospel, God's plan of salvation and righteousness for all men – Jew and Gentile alike (1:16-17). Although justification by faith has been suggested by same as the theme, it would seem that a broader theme states the message of the book more adequately. Righteousness from God (1: 17) includes justification by faith but it also embraces such related ideas as guilt, sanctification and security.

Salvation

This is one of the prominent theological concepts of the epistle of Romans. Salvation is the complete and final purpose of God for the whole person and for all people. Negatively, it involves freedom from all forms of bondage, deliverance from condemnation, removal of alienation. Positively, it implies a new status adoption as sons, consecration and a new quality of life for individual and society.

God did something in Christ, which men on their part were unable to do, but it was not done merely instead of them so that they are freed from the responsibility of doing what they ought to do. Christ is no external representative or substitute. He stands with men and in men. The believer's status as a Christian is not in his hands or in his choice but in the relationship, which he stands with Christ.

Faith

Trust and confidence are the closest words in English, which describes the meaning of faith. It is an acrostic of F = for, A = All, I, T = Trust, H = Him. Generally, the verb which corresponds to faith is to believe, know that something is true or to think or to hope that is true. But Paul uses differently that is believe in, believe on, trust in, rely on etc.

(1) Faith is a human act. It is people who believe.
(2) Faith is called into action by God's power, which works through the gospel (Rom. 1:16) A person cannot have faith independently of God (Eph. 2:8, Phil. 1:29).

(3) When a person believes, God's salvation, which is offered to everyone, becomes effective in his life (1:16, 3:22).

(4) Faith joins us into Christ, so that we are united with Him.

(5) To believe or not to believe is a decision, which each person must make for himself. People will be saved as individuals, not in groups (Matt. 24:40-42). But in fact no man lives alone, as an isolated individual, because people influence one another (Acts 16:33, I Cor. 1: 16).

Sin

This is another theological concept in the epistle of Romans (Rom. 2:12,3:20-25,5:12-6:23,7:7-25,8:2,3). Sin is the name given to any action, word or thought, which goes against God's will. Thus, the most important thing to notice about sin is that it is against God. We may hurt or offend our fellow men, but we sin against God. All the different Greek words used for sin-missing the mark, lawlessness, falling, transgression, unrighteousness, wickedness emphasize this fact. Its results are that it separates men from God and brings God's wrath. Sin in the life of men can be thought of in three ways:

(1) There are sinful actions. A man can sin by thought, word or deed.

(2) There is the power of sin. It is the source or root of men's sinful actions. It sometimes seems as though Paul thought of it as a power outside men, at other times as a corruption or sickness, within men.

(3) There is the guilt of sin. This word comes from the law court and refers to men's status or standing, before God. Those who have disobeyed God's law are sinners. God, as the righteous judge, through His law, declares them to be guilty. He condemns them. They deserve to be punished.

Christology

The whole epistle is the story of God's plan of redemption in Christ. More specifically, Jesus Christ is our savior, who obeyed God perfectly as our representative (5:18,19) and who died as our substitute. Through Christ, we have manifold blessings: reconciliation to God, righteousness and eternal life, identification with Him in His death, burial and resurrection, being alive to God, freedom from condemnation, eternal inheritance. Indeed, all of the Christian life seems to be lived through Him: prayer, rejoicing, exhortation, glorifying God.

Pneumatology

The Holy Spirit gives power in preaching the gospel in working miracles (15:19), dwells in all who belong to Christ and gives us life. He also makes us progressively more holy in daily life, empowering us to obey God and overcome sin (2:29,7:6). The Holy Spirit pours God's love into our hearts (5:5,15:30), along with joy, peace and hope by His power (14:17). He enables us to pray rightly (8:26).

Out Line

1. Sin – universal and incurable 1-3

2. Salvation from sin 3-8

    – Through justification 3-5
    – Through sanctification 6-8

3. Sovereignty of God 9-11

4. Service 12-16

    – The Christian and God 12:2
    – The Christian and the world 12:2
    – The Christian and his fellow Christian 12:3-16
    – The Christian and his enemy's 12:17-21
    – The Christian and the state 13
    – The Christian and weak believers 14, 15
    – Personal messages to the Church of Rome 16

Application

Romans teaches us that we should not trust ourselves for salvation, but in Christ (1-5) that we should imitate the faith of Abraham (4), be patient in times of trouble (5:1-11), rejoicing in our representation by Christ (5:12-21), grow in daily death to sin (6:1-7:25); walk according to the Spirit each moment (8:1-17), hope in future glory and trust that God will bring good out of present sufferings (8:18-39), pray for and proclaim the gospel to the lost, especially the Jews (9:1-11:32) and praise God for His great wisdom in the plan of salvation.(11:33-36).

I CORINTHIANS

Corinth was the capital of the Roman province of Achaia, which was the second largest city in this province. This city was important city in every way. It also enjoyed a commercial advantage. The city was rich economically because it had sea harbors, the center for business and trade. Also many pagan temples and shrines thrived in the city. In fact, at a time when public morality throughout the Roman Empire was at a low level, Corinth was noted for its moral depravity. The very name of the city became a verb which meant 'to be like an immoral life'. There were many taverns and easy access to prostitutes. The society was prosperous and grossly immoral. The moral standard and values were decaying day by day in this city. The apostle Paul came there to preach the Gospel of Jesus Christ about AD 50 or 51. As a result of his Spirit-empowered witness, the church in Corinth was born. Most of its members were Gentiles and from the lower classes (I Cor. 1: 26-31,7:18-24,11:21-22,12:2).

Here, a numbers of converts struggled with the responsibility of being the people of God in the midst of a pagan city. All of them lived under the relentless pressures of a pagan society, which sought, to conferring them to its corrupt way. Thus I Corinthians provides the most intimate disclosure of the inner life and workings of an early congregation.

Probably, 5 years after the establishment of the church at Corinth, the church was riddled with problems, especially in their relationships with one another. These were divisions over leadership, insets, marital problems, believers suing each other, impropriety during Lord's Supper and many more. It was in this spiritual arena that Paul addressed this letter. He wrote from a broken heart, but with the faith and confidence that they would repent and God would heal their church.

Authorship and Date

Apostle Paul was the author of this book. This epistle was written on the third missionary journey and from Ephesus and in the spring of AD55\56. I Corinthians is a source book of answers to church problems in the past and today. This book has been called as '*the doctrine of the cross*' in its social application.

Purpose

In responding to the reports and answering the questions, it was Paul's purpose to rectify certain serious doctrinal and moral sins and irregularities of Christian living, including disorderly conduct in worship. These aberrations included false view of the body (I Cor. 15) incest, adultery and other sexual immorality (I Cor. 5). They also included un-Christian actions in taking fellow Christians to court (6) misuse of Christian liberty (I Cor. 8, 10), disorders in observing the Lord's Supper (I Cor. 11:17-34) and other disorders in the worship service (I Cor. 14). In summary, the main, purpose of this letter was:

1. To correct false doctrines in the church.
2. To help the believers see their sins and weaknesses.
3. To encourage them in having a healthy, mature Christian life.

Theme and Theology

The main theme of I Corinthians is that Jesus Christ and the indwelling Holy Spirit answer all the spiritual problems of Christians and the local churches, where they worship and fellowship.

The letter revolves around the theme of problems in Christians conduct in the church. It then has to do with progressive sanctification, the continuing development of holiness of character.

In one way or another, wrong living always stems from wrong belief. For example: sexual sins, including divorce, are inevitably related to disobeying God's plan for marriage and family (7:1-40). Proper worship is determined by such things as recognition of God's holy character (3:17), the spiritual identity of the church (12:12-27) and pure partaking of the Lord's Supper (11:17-34). It is not possible for the church to be edified faithfully and effectively unless believers understand and exercise their spiritual gifts (12:1-14:40).The doctrine of resurrection of the dead also has been dealt in this epistle. In addition to these theological themes, Paul deals briefly with God's judgment, the right understanding of which will produce right motives for godly living (3:13-15). The right understanding of idols and false gods has been dealt in these epistles.

So Paul deals with the cross, divine wisdom and human wisdom, the work of the Holy Spirit in illumination, carnality, eternal rewards, the transformation of salvation, sanctification, the nature of Christ, union with Him, the divine role of women, marriage and divorce, spirit baptism, indwelling and gifting, the unity of the church in one body, the theology of love, and the doctrine of resurrection. All these establish foundational truth for godly behavior.

Christology

The letter contains an unmatched revelation of the cross of Christ as a center to all-human boasting (ch 1-4). Paul cites Christ as our example in all behavior (11:1) and describes the church as His Body (12). Especially important are the powerful consequences of Christ's resurrection for the whole of creation (15).

Pneumatology

The manifestations or the gifts of the Spirit make up the best-known passages about the Holy Spirit (ch 12-14). The role of the Holy Spirit is shown as the revealer of the things of God to the human spirit (2:1-13).

Out Line

Problems of a local church

1. Introduction 1:1-9

2. Bad Reports 1:10-6:20

    Divisions 1:10-4:23
    Disorders 5:1-6:20

3. Answering question 7:1-15:58

    Personal problems 7:1-11:1
    Public worship problems 11:2-14:40
    Questions about the resurrection 15:1 -58

4. Conclusion 16: 1-24

Application

Christians in Corinth and Christians today share the problems of faction (division) in the church, moral problems, marriage and divorce and other human issues. Because the church is made up of people and people are imperfect, we can expect these kinds of problems in the church. The church was not established for perfect people but for sinners. We must not then be surprised to see sinners and their shortcomings in the church. Rather, we should rejoice that Christ gave us the church where we can help each other through our weaknesses and failures. We must demonstrate the love of Christ to one another (13) and not condemn each other as we seek the truth of God's Word together as brothers and sisters.

The letter of I Corinthians is actually Paul's response to a letter from the Church of Corinth in which they had asked some very specific questions regarding personal and corporate issues. In fact, the resurrected Christ and the indwelling Holy Spirit provide believers with sufficient answers.

II CORINTHIANS

This letter is addressed to the same church as I Corinthians. Apparently, some of the Christians of Corinth began to seriously doubt Paul's authority as an apostle of Christ. After the 1st letter, Paul's travelling companion, Titus made a visit to Corinth to see how they were doing after Paul's first letter (II Cor. 2:12 and 7:5-16). The report that Titus brings back to Paul is somewhat bitter sweet. There has been repentance and growth in many areas, but there is also a group within the church that doesn't respect Paul, so, this letter is Paul's response to the report of Titus.

Authorship and Date

Paul is the author of this letter (1:1,10:1). It is stamped with his style and it contains more autobiographical material than any of his other writings. The available evidence indicates that the year A.D. 55 is a reasonable estimate for the writing of this letter. From I Cor. 16: 5-8, we conclude that I Corinthians was written from Ephesus before Pentecost and that II Corinthians was written later that same year before the onset of winter. II Cor. 2:13,7:5 indicate that it was written from Macedonia.

Purpose

Paul had several overriding purposes in writing. He wished:

1. To express his great relief and delight at the Corinthians' positive response to his severe letter that had been delivered and reinforced by Titus (II Cor. 2: 6,9,12-14).

2. To prepare them for his forth coming visit by having them engage in self-examination and self-judgment (12:14,13:1,5,11) so that they could discover the proper criteria for distinguishing between rival apostles (ch 10-13).

3. To exhort the Corinthians to complete their promised collection for the saints at Jerusalem before his arrival on the next visit (II Cor. 8: 6,7,10,11,9:3-5).

4. There were of course other aims or purposes like to encourage the reaffirmation of their love for the penitent wrongdoers (2:5-11), to insist on their separation from all idolatrous associations (6:14-7:1) and to describe the true nature of his calling of the Christians ministry (2:14-7:4).

Theme and Theology

Traditionally, Paul's two letters to Timothy and one to Titus are called the pastorals. But II Corinthians has a strong claim to be recognized as the pastoral epistle par excellence because it contains not 'pure' but 'applied' *pastoralia*. Paul, the pastor has unconsciously penned a profound, though brief, autobiography. In this epistle, we can see beautiful example of the tenderness of a spiritual shepherd sensitive to the needs of the flock (1:24, 2:6, 7, 6:1, 10:2, 13:5, 10) and also the pleading of a spiritual father jealousy of his children affection, purity and unity (6:11-13, 11:2, 3, 13:11).

The epistle also contains the classic discussion of the theology of Christian suffering (1:3-11, 4:7-18, 6:3-10, 12:1-10), the role of a minister of the new covenant (2:14-17, 4:1-5, 5:16-21), the relation between the old and new covenants (3:7-18) the theology of death and resurrection (4:7-5:10) and the principles and practice of Christian stewardship (II Cor. 8-9)

Christology

Jesus Christ is the focus of our relationship with God. Only in Him, do we see the glory of God and only in Him are we transformed by the glory (3:14,18), for Christ is the very image of God (4:4-6). He became sin for us (5:21) and we became new creation in Him (5:17). Jesus is also the focus of our service to God. We share not only His life and glory but also His dying (4:10). We experience His weakness but also His strength as we seek to bring every thought into captivity to obedience of Christ (10:5). Jesus is the focus of our present life in this world (4:10,11) and Jesus is the focus of our future life, for we will be raised up with Jesus (4:14).

Pneumatology

The Holy Spirit is the power of the new covenant (3: 6) because He makes real to us the present and future provisions of our salvation in Christ. The Holy Spirit helps us to experience and embody the will of God and we ourselves become epistles of Christ, known and read by all men (3: 2). When we submit ourselves to the work of the Spirit, we experience a miracle. The work of the Holy Spirit is evident in daily inward renewal (4:16), spiritual warfare (10:3-5), and the signs, wonders and mighty deeds of Paul's ministry in Corinth (12:12).

Out Line

1. Paul's greetings 1:1-11

2. Paul's ministry 1:12-7:16

3. Paul's collection 8:1-9:15
   The patterns of giving 8:1-9
   The purpose of giving 8: 10-15
   Procedure of giving 8:16-9:5
   The Promise of giving 9:6-15

4. Paul's apostleship 10:1-12:13
   Apostolic authority 10:1-18
   Apostolic conduct 11:1-15
   Apostolic suffering 11:16-33
   Apostolic credentials 12:1-13

5. Paul's visit 12:14-13:14
   Paul's unselfishness 12:14-18
   Paul's warnings 12:19-13:10
   Paul's benediction 13:11-14

Application

Like the Corinthian Christians, each one of us also have areas in our lives that need improvement. II Corinthians gives us encouragement to continue on the path of personal improvement and spiritual growth. Likewise, we need to be sympathetic and encouraging to our fellow Christians who are trying to make positive changes in their lives as well. In addition, we need to exhibit a Christ like concern and understanding of the sacrifices that God's servants make in their work for Christ and His church.

Elders of the church, especially, deserve our respect for their God-given authority and leadership. In truth, all Christians using their special gifts and talents from the Lord should be encouraged to continue praising Him in their unique ways so that, as Paul says in his first letter, we can save some of them (the lost) in any way possible (I Cor. 9: 22).

GALATIANS

The book of Galatians has been conferred with such titles as *the battle cry of the reformation,* and *the Christian's declaration of independence.*

Authorship and Date

Paul clearly states that he is the author of this letter and also indicates that there are a number of brothers in the Lord with him. It is likely that Paul wrote this letter before the Jerusalem Council described in Acts 15, which would make it sometimes in A.D 48. Galatians is one of the few letters written by Paul to a province rather than an individual person or city. Paul clearly wrote to the churches in Galatia, indicating that it was meant for many first readers.

Purpose

Some of Paul's main purposes in writing this epistle were:

1. To expose the false teachings of the Judaizer (faith and work, law and salvation) who were undermining the faith of the new converts.

2. To defend Paul's apostleship, which was being challanged by the Judaizer.

3. To emphasize that salvation is through faith alone, not faith plus law.

4. To exhort the Galatian Christians to live in the liberty brought by Christ (5:10) and bring forth the fruit of the Spirit (5:22-23).

Theme and Message

The theological theme of Galatians is that true freedom comes only through Jesus Christ. In this letter, Paul deals with spiritual freedom on two fronts. The first front (Ch 3-4) is that of salvation, through which Christ sets a person free from bondage to sin and the law. As the apostle declares in the book of Romans "the Law of the Spirit of life in Christ Jesus has set you free from the Law of sin and of death" (8:2). Paul's second front in Galatians (Ch 5-6) is that of sanctification, the freedom God gives His children to live out lives of faithfulness and genuine righteousness, free from sin's control and legalistic bondage.

The message of Galatians is the message of the Christian's spiritual freedom, his deliverance by Christ from the bondage of sin and religious legalism.[15] Its message is particularly revelant in our own day, as personal freedom has became the dominant emphasis of countless philosophies. The message of Galatians was the message of God's grace, of pure grace. A person does not win, earn or merit salvation, a person is saved by the grace of God through His Son, the Lord Jesus Christ.

Special Features

1) Galatia was a district that stretched across the middle of Asia Minor. The native of Galatians were themselves an emotional, and impulsive chargeable people. They were an impetuous, fickle, arguing, boastful, and immoral people. Both Jews and Greeks were residing in the area.

2) The church was spiritually immature.

3) Galatians is the message of liberty, yet subjection; the message of unity, yet diversity; the message of oneness, yet difference.

Christology

Paul teaches that Jesus places those who have faith in Him (2:16,3:26) in a position of liberty (2:4, 5:1) freeing them from bondage to legalism. The apostle's main emphasis is on the crucifixion of Christ as the basis for the believer's deliverance from the curse of sin (1:4, 6:14), self (2:20) and law (3:12,4:5). Paul also describes a dynamic faith-union with Christ (2: 20). Jesus is the substance of the gospel (1:7).

Pneumatology

We receive the Holy Spirit by faith and that Spirit continues to

---

[15] A major wrong use of the Law is called legalism. Relying on obedience to moral law or observance of ceremonial law for salvation (Rom. 3: 20, 28; Gal. 2:16, 3:11) has been the historic theological meaning of legalism. Legalism means -relying on obedience to law for acceptance with God.

manifest Himself in power as we walk in faith. In 5:16-25, Paul graphically describes a fierce and constant conflict between the indwelling Spirit. Only the Holy Spirit can enable us to die to the flesh (vs. 16, 17), deliver us from the tyranny of the law (vv.18) and cause the fruit of the holiness to grow in our lives (vs. 22, 23).

Out Line

1. Personal : Paul's apostolic authority 1-2
    Salvation and introduction 1:1-9
    Apostolic credentials 1:10-24
    Apostolic commendation 2:1-10
    Apostolic confidence 2:11-21

2. Doctrinal: salvation only by grace through faith 3-4
    Confirmed by experience 3:1-5
    Affirmed by scripture 6-4:31

Application

Legalism, which teaches that justification or sanctification depends upon a person's own efforts, thus denying the sufficiency of the cross, is the most persistent enemy of the gospel of grace. Circumcision and other requirements of the Mosaic Law may no longer be issues pertaining to salvation, but often times the observance of certain rules, regulations or religious rites are made to coordinate with faith in Christ, as the condition of Christian maturity. Galatians clearly declares the perils of legalism and establishes the essential truth of salvation by faith alone. There is true liberty only in Christ Jesus. True liberty in Christ is neither the legalism of the law nor the license of the flesh.

PRISON LETTERS

The letters from Ephesians, Philippians, Colossians and Philemon are called the prison letters because they were written from the prison.

EPHESIANS

This was among the last letters which Paul wrote prior to his execution in Rome. It was his loftiest statement about the church. In it, he declared the extensiveness of Christ's love for the church. He was willing to die for it.

Authorship and Date

From the internal evidence, it is clear that Paul wrote this letter around A.D. 61-62 from Rome. It was brought to the first readers by a young man named Tychicus, who also carried Paul's letters to the Colossians and the slave owner Philemon. This letter was probably a circular and the Church of Ephesus was probably the first and last church to read the letter in its circulation. The first readers of Ephesians were a mixture of Jews and Gentiles who had become Christians during Paul's earlier visit.

Purpose

The following are the purposes of Ephesians:

1. To reveal the purpose of God for the whole universe. God has shown His purpose through His Son, Jesus Christ and He is working out His purpose through the church, which is His Body on earth.

(2) To encourage the church to walk in a spirit of oneness and unity to be 'ye kind one to another, tender hearted, forgiving one another' (4:32).

The City of Ephesus

She was the most important city along the coast of Asia Minor. Her attraction was not only her natural harbour, but the rich, fertile land that covered the inland area. She was a great commerical city. The city was rich. The great city of Ephesus had a disease, the disease of sensual unrighteousness and the disease did its work: it corrupted the people. The people, sensual and self-centred, lost their will and willingness to ply a commendable trade. Thus, the disease of Ephesus proved mortal. The lampstand of Ephesus crumbled,and the light of Ephesus died out (Rev. 2:1-7).

Theology

A. Church

The doctrine most extensively treated in the epistle is that of the church-ecclesiology. Three images are used to describe it : the body of Christ (1:23,4;3-16); the bride of Christ (5:22 ff) and the temple of the Holy Spirit (2:19-22). In Ephesians, the concept that best defines the church is the body, of which Christ is head. The community of believers who have received this renewed life by the Holy Spirit constitute His body on earth. Yet, because He fills this body with His own life, He transforms its existance from one that is only earthly to one that is heavenly. This doesn't mean that the church no longer lives an empirical life in this world. It is concerned with this life in the world that caused Paul to write most of his letters to the churches. But it does mean that the ultimate origin, and history of the church can no longer be found in the temporal sphere, but rather in that which is hidden in the eternal purposes of God. Through the church even the angelic powers are to be brought to know the wisdom of God. Therefore, Christ loves the church and labors over her that she may become a vessel worthy to fulfill the purposes of God.

B. Holy Spirit

Another strong theological concept of Ephesians is the concept of Holy Spirit. The Spirit is given to the believer at baptism (1:13), whose presence assures him of his share in the inheritance from the Father (1:14,5:5). He enlightens the believer's mind to make him wise towards God (1:17); furnishes access to the Father (2:18), indwells the community enabling it to became a holy temple of the Lord (2:22); makes the believers strong with the might of God (3:16) and constitutes part of the oneness and unity of the believers (4:4). Christians are admonished not to grieve the Spirit (4:30), urged to be filled with the Spirit (5:18) and instructed to pray as those led by the Spirit.(6:18)

Christology

This epistle is rich is its Christology. Christ is the Redeemer (1:7); He is the resurrected Lord. He is the peacemaker who has reconciled man to God (2:11-18); He is the chief cornerstone; He is the treasure (3:8); He is the indweller of human hearts; He is the victor (4:8-10); He is the model husband, unselfishly giving Himself to enhance His bride – the church (5:25-27, 32); He is the Lord, mighty is battle the resource of strength for His own as they arm for spiritual warfare (6:10).

Pneumatology

In this epistle, Holy Spirit has been revealed widely in various ministries to and through the believers. He is the sealer, authorizing the believers to perceive God's purpose (1:7, 3:5). He is the Spirit of unity desiring to sustain the bond of peace in the body of Christ (4:3,4). He is the giver of the word as a sword for battle and the heavenly assistant given to aid us in prayer and intercession until victory is won (6:17and 18).

Message

The letter focuses on what God did through the historical work of Jesus Christ and does through His Spirit today, in order to build His new society in the midst of the old. We, who are in Christ, organically united to Him by faith and have been raised from spiritual death, exalted to heaven and seated with Him there. We have also been reconciled to God and to each other. As a result, through Christ, and in Christ, we are nothing less than God's new society, the single new humanity which He is creating and which includes Jews and Gentiles on equal terms. We are the family of God, the Father, the body of Jesus Christ, His Son and the temple or dwelling place of the Holy Spirit.

Therefore, we are to demonstrate plainly and visibly by our new life- the reality of this new thing which God has done: first by the unity and diversity of our common life, secondly, by the purity and love of our everyday behaviour, next by the mutual submissiveness and care of our relationships at home and lastly by our stability in the fight against the principalities and powers of evil. Then in the fullness of time, God's purpose of unification will be brought to completion under the headship of Jesus Christ.

Out Line

1.   Introduction 1:1-2

2.   Our heritage in Christ 1;3-3:21
     Spiritual blessing in Christ 1:3-14
     Prayer for spiritual wisdom 1:15-23
     Once dead, now alive 2:1-22
     Paul's testimony and prayer 3:1-21

3.   Our life in Christ 4:1-6:20
     Keeping church unity 4:1-16
     Daily Christian living 4:17-5:20
     Christian behavior in the home 5;21-6:9
     The Christians armor 6:10-20

4.   Conclusion 6:21-24

Application

Ephesians discloses awesome blessings of grace (1:6) and awesome dimensions of spiritual authority over evil (3:20). But this awaits the believers first accepting the disciplines of unity (4:1-16), purity (4:17-31), forgiveness (4:32) and walking in the fullness of the Holy Spirit (5:1-21). With this, relationships at every point must be in order (5:22-6:9), the idea being firmly established that true spiritual power flows from true obedience to the divine order in relationships and personal conduct. The believer as the member of the body of Christ is seated in heavenly places in Christ, but yet is to walk in practical love on earth.

PHILIPPIANS

Philippians is the loveliest letter Paul ever wrote. It has been called the *Epistle of Excellent Things* and so indeed it is ; and the *Epistle of Joy*. Again and again the words 'joy' and 'rejoice' recur. Rejoice, writes Paul, again I will say rejoice, even in prison directing the hearts of his friends and ours to the joy that no man can take from us.

Philippians, more than most other epistles of the apostle Paul, reveals Paul's situation, his personal history and his deep and abiding affection for the church that loved him. In addition to revealing Paul's heart, the epistle contains a fresh presentation of Jesus Christ, who changed his life drastically.

Authorship and Date

Paul states himself clearly as the writer of this letter in the opening verse. Timothy was apparently with him in Rome when it was written. Paul was under house arrest at this time, which meant he was still incarcerated, but under minimun security. Philippians was written sometimes between A.D. 61-62.

Purpose

Some members of the church had shown a tendency towards disunity and contentiousness, Paul encouraged them to consider the mind of Christ (2:1-11) and urged them to practice the humility evident in Christ as they related to one another. The church faced a challenge from false teachers who diluted or added to God's way for salvation (3:1-6) Paul made his readers aware of the danger of legalism, on the one hand and the dangers of sensuality and materialistic greed on the other hand. Each of these teachings required strong resistance, and Paul intended to help the church deal with himself (2:19-24). The main purpose of the epistle was to encourage the believers to put Christ first in everyday living; the Christ – centred life.

Theme

Christological hymn (2:6-11), sanctification and the concept of joy are the main theological themes of the letter. While providing a magnificent description of Jesus Christ- pre-existent, equal with God, becoming incarnate, a human being, a servant, totally obedient to God, in turn exalted by God to the highest place in heaven or on earth, the object of worship for all created beings to the glory of God,the Father- this hymn (2:6-11) also articulately describes who God really is. For Jesus Christ, who shared the very nature of God and acted out of that nature, showed by what He chose to do and by what He, in fact did that God's true nature is not characterized by seizing, grasping or attaining, but rather by sharing, by open-handed giving and by pouring oneself out for others in order to enrich them.

The doctrine of sanctification is found in 3:8-16. Holiness described here is an ever-increasing apprehension of the surpassing worth of Jesus Christ by the Christians, with nothing whatsoever allowed to destroy or diminish this apprehension. In turn, it is also an apprehension of the Christians by Jesus Christ. Both elements are present in the work of God or Christ and in the work of the Christians. Sanctification for Paul, therefore, allows room for growth increase, advancement and progress on the part of the Christians (1:9, 25).

Finally, the theme of joy that runs throughout Philippians has had a profound influence on Christians through the centuries. Here one learns that joy is not so much a feeling as it is a settled state of mind characterized by peace, an attitude that views life including all of its ups and down. It is a confident way of looking at life that is rooted in faith in the living Lord of the church (1:25, 3:1, 4:4, 10). For Paul, joy is an understanding of existence that makes it possible for one to accept both elation and depression, to accept with creative submission events that bring either delight or dismay, because joy allows one to see beyond any particular event to the sovereign Lord who stands above all events.

Pneumatology

1. The Holy Spirit will direct the accomplishment of God's purpose (1:19).

2. He promotes unity and fellowship in the body of Christ (2:1).

3. In contrast to the lifeless rituals observance or formalities, the Holy Spirit inspires and directs the worship of true believers (3:3).

Out Line

1. Greetings 1:1-2
2. Paul's joyful response in the difficult circumstance 1;12-26
3. Paul's joyful concern for the church 1:3-11
4. Paul's personal plea for Christian unity and humility 1:27-2:18

5. Paul's pastoral commendation 2:19-30
6. Paul's warning against the error of self-righteousness 3:1-11
7. Paul's single minded exhortation 3:12-4:1
8. Paul's gentle advice for joy and peace 4:2-9
9. Paul's genuine thanksgiving 4:10-20
10. Conclusion 4:21-23

Application

This letter reveals the timeless message that true joy is to be found only in a dynamic personal relationship with Jesus Christ and in the assurance that God is able to turn adverse circumstances to our good and His glory.

Note on Philippians and the Church

Philippi was the Roman province. It was inhabited predominantly by Romans but many Macedonian Greeks and some Jews lived there as well. The people were proud of their city, proud of their tie with Rome, proud to observe Roman customs and obey Roman laws, proud to be Roman citizens (Acts 16:21). Choosing Philippi as the place to launch the gospel on European soil filted in with Paul's mission strategy of selecting important cities of repute and strategic location as ideas centres from which the good news of the gospel might radiate out.

Paul came to Philippi as the result of a vision he had while he was in Troas. He saw a man of Macedonia and heard him say- *'come over..and help us '* (Acts 16:9-10) According to the Acts, the first convert to Christianity in Philippi was a woman, Lydia. Although she was a pagan, she nevertheless was a God-fearing person who had been attracted to the lofty ideals of the Jewish religion (Acts 16:14). But when she heard Paul preach the gospel, God opened her heart, she put her faith in Jesus Christ and along with her household was baptized (16:14-15). These people became the nucleus of the church at Philippi.

COLOSSIANS

Colossians, one of Paul's shortest letters, was written to the infant church at Colossae in the Lycus valley of the province of Asia. This Christian community had not been founded by Paul but came into existence during his Ephesian ministry through the efforts of Epaphras, one of his colleagues.

Authorship and Date

Once again, Paul claims authorship and states that Timothy is present with him at its composition. We have already seen that Philippians, Ephesians and Colossians were all written at about the same time from the same place-house arrest in Rome. The date of this prison epistle is around A.D. 61.

Purpose

The main purpose of this beautiful epistle was to combat an extremely dangerous and threatening heresy that was arising in the Colossian Church. Docetism and Cerinthinism were two threatening heresies in the Colossian Church. According to Docetism, Christ was not really human. He only appreared human. The word docetism means 'to seem'. Jesus only seemed to have a body. He was never really flesh and blood. He came to earth only as a pure spiritual being. According to Cerinthinism, there was a clear distinction between the human and the divine Christ. This just had to be, for God could never suffer and die. He could not really be God if He suffered and died. Thus, it was claimed that the Spirit of God Himself did not enter Jesus untill His baptism and He left Jesus right before His death.

Theology

Paul's major teaching centered around the question; who is Jesus Christ? The apostle insisted that no chasm existed between the transcendent God and His material creation. Christ is both the Creator and Reconciler (1:15-23). He is the exact expression of God and brings together heaven and earth. A hierarchy of angelic powers or ruling spirits to mediate between God and humans is unnecessary. Christ is fully divine and fully human (2:9-10).

Second, he dealt with the issue of genuine spirituality. Paul developed the basis for genuine worship and spirituality by refuting the false spirituality that encouraged an unspiritual pride (2:6-23). He exhorted the Colossians to abandon sins of the old life and cultivate the virtues of the new life (3:5-4:6).

Message

The theme of this letter centers on the supremacy of Christ. In his letter, Paul emphasizes that Christ was sufficient for the total Christian life from beginning to end. Only He is worthy of worship and obedience, for the fullness of God is in Him and in Him alone (1:15-20). Believers needed no other source of understanding and knowledge (2:2).

The worship of the principalities and power-if intermediaries – is both evil and foolish, for Christ is supreme in His authority over all of them (1:16). The unity and growth of the church depended on its faithful relationship to Christ, who is its head (2:19).

Paul wrote this letter to the Colossians to encourage them to remain true to Christ and to assure them that they had in Him all that they needed to live and grow in faith.

Pneumatology

Colossians has a single explicit reference to the Holy Spirit, used in association with love (1:8). Paul says like this – "the Lordship of Christ in the believers life is the most crucial and clearest evidence of the Spirit's presence."

Out Line

1. Introduction 1;1-14
2. Explanation of the supremacy of Christ 1:15-23
3. Ministry for the church 1:24-2:5
4. Warning against false spirituality 2:6-3:4
5. Exhortatians for ethical living 3:5-4:6
6. Conclusion 4:7-18

Application

Because this is an age of religious pluralism and syncretism, Christ's Lordship is deemed irrelevant by many religious groups that believe on religion is as good as the other. Neither the church nor the individual believer can afford to compromise Christ's deity. In His sovereignty lies His sufficiency. He will be Lord of every thing or not Lord at all. Christ is in all, through all and above all. He is the fullness of Godhead bodily and the church is complete in Him.

GENERAL LETTERS

I and II letters of Paul to Thessalonians, Hebrews, James and Jude are the special letters which are known as the general letters in the New Testament.

I THESSALONIANS

On his second missionary journey, Paul and his companions, Silas and Timothy, came from Philippi to Thessalonica and founded the Christian church there. The congregation was largely Gentile Christian although Aristarchus, a Jewish Christian is specifically mentioned in Acts 20:4, Colossians 4:10ff.

Authorship and Date

Paul claims authorship at the very outset of the letter (1:1). Timothy and Silas were with him when he wrote. Paul wrote this letter from Corinth around A.D. 51-52, after the letter to the Galatians, making I Thessalonians his earliest letter to an individual church.

Purpose

Following are the main purposes of this letter:

1. To encourage to face the persecution.
2. To warn them about sexual immorality.
3. To instruct the believers about personal holiness.
4. To give clear-cut instruction about how the Lord's return relates to the life and death of Christians.

Theme and Theology

1. Paul indicates in this epistle that there is one true God as in contrast to all pagan deities (I Thess. 1:9). It is from this one true and living God that the gospel which they declared derived

(2:2). It was to this same God they ultimately were to submit themselves for approval of their labor (2:4,10). This God is the one who providentially directed their lives (3:11). He was the one who would perfect them at the coming of Christ (5:23). This God is faithful to accomplish the work which He had began (5:24).

2. As far as the Christology is concerned, the apostle unites the Son with the Father as to indicate clearly His essential equality with the Father (1:1).

3. As respects the doctrine of the Holy Spirit (pneumatology), the apostle teaches that it is the Spirit who makes the message effective in the heart of hearers (1: 5). It is the Spirit who gives joy in affliction (1:6). God gives the Holy Spirit to all believers (4:7ff), therefore, they must be careful not to fall into uncleanliness.

4. As respects of soteriology, the apostle mentions the great doctrine of redemption through the death of Christ only once (5:10).

5. The doctrine of eschotology.[16] It is from the futuristic perspective that the 'obtaining of salvation' is primarily conceived in the Thessalonian epistles. In 1 Thessalonians there is mention of the Parousia in each chapter, with extensive discussion in ch. 4, 5.

Pneumatology

The Spirit inspires joy even amid affliction (1:6). 1 Thess 5:19-21 reveals a lively charismatic character to the worship at Thessalonians prophetic activity, which some were inclined to subdue, but for which Paul asks tested acceptance: his words were to be read to all the holy brethren (5:27).

---

[16] Eschatology is traditionally defined as the doctrine of the last things (Greek *'eschata'*) – in relation either to the individual human being (in which case they comprise death, resurrection, judgment and the after life) or to the world.

Message

The letter is more practical than theological. It is God – centered (theo-centric) throughout. God chose the Thessalonians unto salvation (1:4). His will is the guide for all believers (4:3). He calls His people to holy living (4:7) and enables them to live obediently, He raised Jesus from the dead (4:14) and will raise believers to be with Him at the Lord's return (4:13-5:11).

Out Line

1. Greeting 1:1

2. Looking back 1:2-3:13

    Conversion and Testimony 1:2-:16
    Paul's service to them 2:17-3:13

3. Looking forward 4:1-5:24

    Their daily walk 4:2-12
    The Lord's return 4:13-5:24

4. Conclusion 5:25-28

Application

Concerning the second coming of Jesus Christ, two things are certain: 1).The return of Christ is an assured future event. 2).That event is closer than it has ever been before. But to specify a date for the second coming or to specify time by which the Lord must surely return, or to focus solely on detailed prophetic systems that attempt to sequence precisely various final events described in scripture – such efforts dilute the force of Christ's return as revealed in I Thessalonians.

II THESSALONIANS

After Paul wrote I Thessalonians some of the people in the church got the wrong understanding about his teaching on the coming *'day of the Lord'* in the clouds to take up (rapture), the saints, dead and living, to heaven (I Thess. 4:13-18). Then the Thessalonians spread the word that 'the day' had already come (II Thess. 2:2) and that 's why they were experiencing persecution (1:4). There was even the strong probability that some one had written to the church with these teaching, claiming to be Paul (2:1-2).

Paul wanted to correct these wrong beliefs by saying that the time of eternal punishment was yet to come (1:7-10). So, he wrote a second letter to the Church in Thessalonica.

Authorship and Date

Paul's name appears twice in this letter, claiming authorship in both places (1:1). He probably wrote this second letter about six months after the first one, which would place it around A.D. 52 from Corinth.

Purpose

i.   He wrote this letter to encourage the persecuted church (1:4-10)

ii. He attempted to correct their misunderstanding about the Lord's return.

iii. He exhorted the church to be steadfast in all things (2:13-3:15).

iv. Without being disturbed and confused, the believers of Thessalonica should stand strong and continue to believe the teachings he gave them and work productively in the meantime (1:3-10,2:13-17, 3:6-15).

Theology

God is viewed as the true author of all grace and peace (1:2;2:16, 3:16). It is before Him that the highest human hopes will be consummated (2:19).

Christ is so united with the Father as to leave no doubt concerning His essential equality and hence true deity. It is in the Lord Jesus Christ, as well as 'in God, the Father' that the church's life consists (1:1,2).The Spirit's distinctive work is that of sanctification (2:13). The major emphasis of this epistle is eschatological. There is a future time of judgment coming when God will settle His accounts (1:5-10).

Pneumatology

The Spirit's sanctifying work can be seen as one way to view the intent of God for His people is saving them. Prophetic utterance from the Spirit or alleged to be so (2:2) must always be tested (I Thess. 5:20).

Message

The emphasis of the epistle on the second coming of Christ reminds us to be ready for Christ's coming at any time. Likewise, we must be alert to the evil schemes of the man of lawlessness. The church gains strength from the instruction about the wicked activity of Satan with his power and pretended signs and wonders. Believers are empowered with the truth that the man of lawlessness will be finally destroyed by the Lord Jesus at His coming (2:12). In the mean time, the church must remain faithful and steadfast to the goodwill and providential purposes of God.

Out Line

1. Salvation 1:1-2
2. Encouragement for the church 1:3-12
3. Instructions to correct misunderstandings 2:1-12
4. Injunctions to steadfastness 2:13-3:18

Application

Before novel teachings that originated with charismatic prophecy are adopted, they should be tested carefully in the light of the Word of God (I Thess. 5:19-20). It is sobering to learn that even the man of sin, the Antichrist,[17] will posses miraculous powers. Miracles, surprisingly are never a sufficient ground for faith (Matt. 7:21-23; John 2:23-25). But the enduring love of God, which is poured out in the hearts of believers by the Holy Spirit (Rom. 5:5), continues into eternity even after charismatic gifts have passed (I Cor. 13:8-13). Love, then, is the way believers experience eternity within time.

---

[17] 'Anti' can mean either someone who opposes or someone who takes the place of Christ. The Antichrist opposes Christ by seeking to take His place. He is also known as the man of lawlessness.

PASTORAL LETTERS

The three letters, I and II Timothy and Titus stand in very close relationship with one another. In contrast to the other Pauline letters except for Philemon, were written to churches, these three letters were written to fellow workers of the apostle Paul to give instruction concerning their pastoral duties. The similar content of the three letters also binds them together as a special group among the Pauline letters.

They make up a special group and as such contains instructions for the conduct of the pastoral office and has led to the collective designation of these three letter as '*the Pastoral Epistles*'. These epistles are highly being regarded as 'the regulation of ecclesiastical discipline'.

I TIMOTHY

After 3 years of ministry in Ephesus and surrounding areas, Paul returned to Jerusalem. Soon, he was sent to prison in Rome (Acts 21:18-28:31). While there, he sent the Ephesian Church, a letter praising the people for their holy walk with the Lord (Eph. 1:15-16). But soon, Paul began to hear reports of problems that were hurting the churches in that area. After he was released from prison, Paul and Timothy visited the churches around Ephesus and saw the problems, firsthand. Paul asked Timothy to stay on at Ephesus and shepherd the Christians there, working out the problems in the process (1:3). Because he would not be able to reach Ephesus when planned, Paul wrote to his young helper (Timothy).

Authorship and Date

Paul is the author of this epistle. The place of this epistle's origination is uncertain but somewhere in Macedonia seems to be the most likely location (1:3). This letter was written probably sometimes between A.D.63 and 67.

Purpose

(i) To encourage Timothy in his role of training leaders. Paul wants to help him – keep going.

(ii) To warn Timothy. Paul wants Timothy to be aware of the types of false teachers around and the methods they use.

(iii) To instruct Timothy on how a church ought to function, including the role of women, the selection of leadership and the care of widows.

Theology

The letter to Timothy develops a theology of the church. The church needs organization to do its work effectively. Church leaders give guidance and enable the Christian community to carry out its service. The church is to be a pillar and bulwark, a custodian of the truth. The church must always strive to avoid heresy and to teach the truths of the gospel to succeeding generation.

Pneumatology

Direct references to the Holy Spirit in I Timothy are rare, but He was at work from the inception of the Church at Ephesus (Acts 19:1-7). The 'intercessions' (I Tim. 2:1) are prayers that involve the Holy Spirit's assistance (Rom. 8:26, 27). The statement that 'the Spirit expressly says' (Rom. 8:26, 27) underscores the continuing activity of the Holy Spirit.

Out Line

i.   Introduction 1:1-2
ii.   Warning against false Teachers 1:3-20
iii. Guidelines for church worship 2:1-15
iv.   Instructions for church leadership 3:1-13
v.   Maintaining the truth 3:14-4:16
vi.   Personal charge to Timothy 6:11-21

II TIMOTHY

This is the last letter Paul wrote, it is tender and loving. Paul was an old man, living out his final hours in a cold, dark, Roman dungeon. II Timothy is his ' dying wish ' to his faithful friend and co-worker, Timothy.

During the time of its composition, Paul was no longer a freeman. Christians throughout the Roman Empire were now suffering for their faith. The cruel Nero was hostile towards the followers of Jesus. He had the church's dauntless leader Paul behind bars and was planning his imminent death. Tradition tells us that Paul was kept in the infamous Mamertine prison, probably in solitary confinement. It is clear from this letter that he expected to be killed (4:6).

Authorship and Date

Paul clearly states that he is the author of this letter because we know that the Emperor Nero died in June, A.D. 68, it is likely that this letter can be dated prior to that. A.D. 67 is generally the accepted date for its writing.

Purpose

Paul wrote out of a lonely heart, saying a genuine and warm 'good bye' to one who was perhaps his dearest son and friend. His main spiritual purpose was to stimulate, inspire and challenge Timothy to keep going with the gospel ministry.

Theology

Christian workers approved by the Lord endure problems, avoid evil people, make known the good news and teach the Word of God. This second letter to Timothy teaches us about the importance of our theological heritage (1:14). Paul had much to say about what God has done in Christ, our saviour, Jesus Christ has been revealed, has destroyed death and has given us life and immortality (1:8-10).The foundation of the Christian life is what God has already done for us in Christ. We should live boldly, for we have received a Spirit of power, of love and of self-discipline (1:7). These truths about the gospel and Christian living are available to us in God's inspired scripture (3:15-17). Now, we, like Timothy, should pass on these truths to faithful men and women who can also teach others (2:2).

Pneumatology

The Holy Spirit has given Timothy a gift and Paul exhorted him to use it actively (1:6). Furthermore, the Holy Spirit gives power, love and a sound mind (1:7). The indwelling Holy Spirit enables us to be faithful to the gospel committed to us and to safeguard its purity (1:13,14).

Out Line

1. Introduction 1:1-7
2. Suffering and the gospel 1:8-18
3. Encouragement to faithfulness 2:1-13
4. Contrasts in the church 2:14-26
5. Godlessness in the last days 3:1-9
6. Final advice to Timothy 3:10-4:18
7. Final greetings 4:19-22

TITUS

Because of the similarity to I Timothy, it is very likely that Paul wrote these two letters within a short time of one another. He probably wrote Titus around A.D. 62., while enroute to the city of Nicopolis in northern Macedonia, where he was hoping to spend the winter (3:12). Although the letter is addressed to Titus, like I Timothy, we may assume that Paul had a wider audience in mind as well (2:1, 3:1) namely the Cretan Church.

Purpose

Following are the main purposes of Titus:

1   To remind Titus that his task is to supervise the churches.
2   To encourage the Cretan Christians about doing good deeds in everyday living.

Theology

Like the other pastoral letters, Paul's letter to Titus focuses on keeping the faith and refuting heresy.[18] The letter makes it plain that the Christian life is grounded in the grace of God (2:11-14).

Believers must recognize this truth and rebuke heresy and avoid legalism (1:10-16). This can be done only by grace – grace that saves, grace that teaches, grace that strengthens and grace that enables. In doing so, we can see the relationship between doctrine and practice.

Pneumatology

The ministry of the Holy Spirit is understood throughout the entire epistle. The Cretans cannot change themselves (1:12,13), and regeneration can only be the work of the Holy Spirit in order to maintain a victorious life-style patterned after that of Christ (3:6-8).

Out Line

1. Introduction 1:1- 4
2. The appointment of elders 1:5-9
3. The rebuke of false teachers 1:10-16
4. The diffent groups in the Christian living 3:1-11
5. The responsibility request 3:12-15
6. Personal concluding request 3:12-15

Theme

The Gospel

In all three of the pastoral epistles,[19] a concern for the truth of the gospel is a powerful influence. Paul uses both the courtroom image of justification and the social image of redemption to describe the results of responding to the Gospel. Gospel should be responded by faith.

---

[18] The Greek word heresy means 'a choice' (Lev. 22:18,21) ; a sect or party (holding certain opinion) ; a sect or faction within the Christian body. Heresy is a deliberate denial of revealed truth coupled with the acceptance of error.

[19] The word comes directly from the Greek word "epistolē". It is the regular word for a letter. Frankly speaking, a letter is actually written from one person or group to another person or group whereas an epistle is in the form of a letter but is meant for general circulation. In fact, all the books called

Church Government

Paul pictures the church in the pastoral epistles as a united family, ministering to its constituency and organized for service. The church is the family of God, and believers are brothers and sisters. Paul charged the church with a responsibility of the poor and to serve as a foundation of doctrinal and ethical truth. Women also filled a special position of service in the church.

Heresy

In the second century, Christianity became involved in a fierce struggle with a heretical movement known as Gnosticism.[20] This false teaching denied the resurrection of Christ, vacillated between moral license and rigid asceticism and insisted that sinful human beings could not enjoy fellowship and full contact with the transcendent God. The heresy, Paul describes here was characterized by an interest in Jewish Law (I Tim. 1:6-7) and showed the influence of 'those of the circumcision group' (Titus 1 :10).

Salvation

Pastoral epistles recognize the universal problem of sin and God's desire to redeem humanity from sin's power and penalty. Both God and Jesus Christ are referred to as saviour throughout the pastorals. Paul boldly asserts that Christ Jesus came into the world to save sinners (I Tim. 1:15). Salvation is God's work alone, promised by God before the beginning of time, and historically realized at His appointed season (Titus 1:3). Believers are referred to as Christ's

---

epistles and all the epistles mentioned in the New Testament are letter in the fullest sense.

[20] It is the very dangerous heresy, cult or false teaching which came into the church like a flood in the second century. The term gnostic comes from the Greek word *gnosis* which means 'knowledge'. Their main teachings was like this : All matter is evil. In order to save the human beings from this evil world, a secret spiritual knowledge is essential which saves them. They taught and badly propogated that the historical Christ was a mere man, but he was taken over by the heavenly Christ who was the brightest of all aeons. This heavenly Christ acted in the man Jesus but was never incarnate. He could not be, because matter was so evil. The heavenly Christ returned to heaven before the crucifixion, so it was only a man called Jesus who died on the cross.

elect, as redeemed through Christ's self- sacrifice and can be described as saved, reborn, renewed and justified (Titus 3:5-7).

The Trinity

Paul describes God, the Father by reference to His attributes and His actions. He portrays God as living and as observing the moral actions of His creatures. Paul refers to God as eternal, immortal invisible and as the holy God. He reflects monotheism by his reference to God as one. The majesty of God is such that He is unapproachable, deserving blessing and thanksgiving from His creatures. God is also faithful and truthful to His promise, merciful in salvation and generous in giving the Holy Spirit. Paul also describes God as Creator and Bestower of life. He is the sovereign ruler who has condescended to reveal Himself in scripture. The course of all history is in His hands.

Application

(1) The pastorals provide insight

They help us in dealing with contemporary problems of heresy, divisionnness and leadership difficulties. They are not a collection of rigid rules for church organization, but guidelines, which provide direction for facing problems, and church needs.

(2) The pastorals are realistic

They present the churches Paul founded with all their needs, weaknesses and shortcomings (I Tim. 4: 1-3). However, they also present the mighty power of God as a prescription for human failure (I Tim. 1:17) and they show His divine power at work in the lives of people (I Tim. 1 : 12-17).

(3) The pastorals provide encouragement

Most of the time Paul remain steadfastly optimistic (II Tim. 4: 6-8). He was lonely, but he was vigilant, irrepressibly a preacher, confident in the Lord. The pastorals provide a picture of the earthly church as it faced error, greed and moral corruption. In spite of these shortcomings, there is a clear sign of anticipated victory and hopeful moral restitution. Churches today need a heavy dose of such realism and encouragement.

The Man Called Timothy

Timothy was a young man who had joined Paul on his second missionary journey when he was in the city of Lystra in Galatians. Timothy's mother, Eunice, was a Jew and his father a Greek. He was with him (Paul) in Rome when he wrote his four prison letters. By and large, this young man was Paul's right hand. There is even good evidence that Paul was the one who led Timothy to the Lord (I Tim. 1: 2 ; II Tim. 1: 2; I Cor. 4: 17). Paul calls him a spiritual son.

The Man Called Titus

Titus was the inhabitant of Crete. Paul and Titus must have done evangelistic work in towns on the Island of Create, South of Greece (1:5). So, Titus was a young, gifted co-worker of Paul, probably even converted under the apostle's ministry (I Tim 1:2; Titus 1:4). He served as Paul's representative in difficult churches on the Mediterranean. We can assume that he was a competent and loyal disciple of Christ or Paul would never have left him in charge of a group of churches. Paul says Cretans are always liars, evil brutes, lazy, gluttons (1:12).

PHILEMON

Philemon was a wealthy, slave owner who had been converted under Paul's ministry in Ephesus. Onesimus was one of his slaves. Onesimus concluded that, since he had no rights under the law, he had no responsibility either. So he ran away. Ultimately, in Rome, he found Paul whom he chose to serve. But Paul, after leading him to repentance and faith, encouraged him to return to his owner. In the letter, Paul urged Philemon to receive Onesimus as a brother in Christ.

Authorship and Date

Paul wrote the letter, sending Timothy greetings in its opening verse. The apostle was still under house arrest in Rome during his first imprisonment there, making the date very near to that of the other prison epistles, A.D. 61. The letter has Philemon as its primary recipient, but Paul also sent greetings to Philemon's wife Apphia, their son, Archippus and to the church that met in their home. This letter gives us a tiny glimpse into the dynamics of a first century household.

Purpose

Paul's primary purpose was to seek to secure Onesimus' reinstatement, as a brother in the Lord, in the household of Philemon from which he had fled.

Theology

Paul's request to Philemon concerning Onesimus is parallel to Christ's request to the Father concerning the fallen humanity, the slave of the devil.

Message

The primary message of this epistle is Christian fellowship. Fellowship is participation in the lives of others partner's lives interrelated at the deepest levels and this partnership became the main avenue of appeal from Paul to Philemon. Another powerful message is the expression of Christian thought in action. This epistle provides insight into Paul that no other does. Paul pondered the meaning of grace, the cross and the nature of salvation. Apart from personal salvation, nothing equals Christ' likeness in attitudes and actions. The gospel demands it. In the epistle, Paul demonstrated it.

Christology

This epistle powerfully applies the message of the gospel. Once a strangled slave is now a beloved in Christ as well (v. 16). Paul's offer to pay a debt that was not his own on behalf of a repentant slave is a clear picture of the work of calvary. Paul's intercession is furthermore analogous to Christ's ongoing intercession with the Father on our behalf.

Pneumatology

It is the Holy Spirit who baptizes all believers, whether slave or free, into the body of Christ (I Cor. 12:13). Paul applies this truth to the lives of Philemon and Onesimus. Love, a fruit of the Spirit is evident throughout the letter.

Out Line

1.   The salutation v.v 1-3
2.   Prayer of thanksgiving v.v 4-7
3.   A good word on behalf of Onesimus v.v 8-21
4.   Paul's personal request v. 22
5.   Greetings and benediction v.v 23-25

Application

This work presents the incredible power of Christ to bring healing to broken lives. It includes the personal reunion between Jesus Christ and the runaway sinner, as well as the wonderful restoration of two believers who were formerly separated. Only with Christ's example of forgiveness, through the cross, are we able to overcome our hurts and mistakes and be reconciled to our brother and sisters in Christ. Regardless of our social position, we are all brothers and sisters in the Lord.

HEBREWS

Although Hebrews is often called a letter, only its closing resembles this form of communication. It is better to think of Hebrew as an essay or treatise that develops its argument point by point. At the same time, its closing does remind us of the closing verses of Paul's letters. This observation urges us to read Hebrews, like the other New Testament materials, as a document written to address particular people, facing particular issues at a particular time.

Authorship and Date

No one is certain about who wrote this book. Different possibilities have been suggested, including Paul, Barnabas, Apollos and others. Still, it is safest and just to refer to the author as 'the writer of Hebrews'. The likely recipients of this letter were Jewish Christians, outside of Palestine, who were being tempted by Judaizers to become another Jewish sect. It was written from Rome/Italy. Since it appears the temple was still standing and the sacrificial system was still in use (10:2,3,11), the letter was probably written before A.D. 70. It may have been composed during the time of Emperor Nero's persecution of Christians about A.D. 64, with the suffering mentioned in 10:32-34.

Purpose

This letter was written to encourage and exhort scattered Jewish Christians to persevere in their faith, in spite of persecution. It warns them not to retreat in to a displaced and inferior Jewish legal and sacrificial system. It argues passionately for the superiority of Christ over the old system, pointing out how he accomplished once for all people and all time what the fulfilled older system could never do.

Theme

Hebrews show Jesus' fulfillment of the sanctuary, sacrifices and priesthood established in the Law of Moses. The writer of Hebrews quotes extensively from the Greek Old Testament (LXX) to show the limitations of the law and its sacrificial system. He also shows how the law points to a new high Priest- Jesus Christ. He says Christ is better than the mediators, sanctuary, and sacrifices under the law. He is worthy of more honor than Moses (3:3). The way of the Law has been superseded by the way of faith in Christ (Ch 11), and there is no turning back from the superior to the inferior.

Christology

The writer emphasizes the superiority of Christ to all who have gone before in Old Testament times. Like no other book in the Bible, Hebrews points out the importance and the ministry of the pre – incarnate Christ.

Pneumatology

The ministry of the Holy Spirit is seen in a variety of ways, applying to both the Old Testament and New Testament periods: gifts of the Holy Spirit for ministry (2:4), witness to the inspiration of the Old Testament (3:7, 10:15), descriptive of the experience of believers (6:4), interpreting spiritual truth (9:8), assisting in the ministry of Jesus (9:14), insulted by apostasy[21] (10:29).

---

[21] It is a doctrinal departure by professed believers who have never been regenerated and who deliberately reject the cardinal Christian rules of Christ's

Out Line

1. The superiority of Christ Jesus' Person 1:1-4:13
    Better than the prophets 1:1-3
    Better than the angels 1:4-2:18
    Better than Moses 3:1-19
    Better than Joshua 4:1-13

2. The superiority of Christ Jesus' ministry 4:4-10:18
    Better than Aaron 4:14-5:10
    The Melchizedek priesthood 7:1-8:5
    Jesus mediates a better covenant 8:6-10:18

3. The superiority of the walk of faith 10:19-13:25
    A call to full assurance of faith 10:19-11:40
    The endurance of faith 12:1-29
    Admonitions of love 13:1-17

4. Conclusion 13:18-25

Application

Christianity is not something added on to Judaism. It is something new, but a fuller understanding of the old covenant gives a richer and more marvellous appreciation of the new covenant of God's grace through our Lord, Jesus Christ. Faith in the blood of our eternal, perfect and heavenly Priest is better than that which was shadowed forth in the old covenant.

JAMES

James is a highly practical book dealing with faulty teaching and behavior. It exhorts the scattered Jewish believers to live consistent lives. Opening with a discussion of trials and temptations, James proceeds to a strong case for a faith that exhibits good works. Other topics covered in this book include favoritism and the misuse of the tongue, earthly versus heavenly wisdom, quarrels and slanders.

---

deity and redemptive sacrifice (I John 4:1-3; II Pet 2:1). Apostasy is irremediable and waits divine judgment (II Pet 2:1 -3).

Authorship and Date

James, the half brother of the Lord is the author of this book (1:1). This book was written to Jewish Christians scattered from Judæa because of the persecution that arose after the stoning of Stephen (Acts 8:1). It is likely that, since James was the leader of the church in Jerusalem, this book was written from there. Since no mention is made of the circumstances that led to the Council of Jerusalem, the book was probably written between A.D.44 - 49.

Purpose

James is primarily practical and ethical, emphasizing duty rather than doctrine. The book was written to encourage persecuted Jewish Christians to live as Jesus taught. There are many parallels in this book to Jesus' Sermon on the Mount (Matt. 5-7). James offers practical advice for Christian living, with special attention given to class divisions in the church and the abuse of the tongue. Prayer is held out as the only way to receive wisdom, the meeting of needs or healing.

Theme

James weaves together three primary themes:

(1) James has a great deal to say about wealth and poverty and especially about the importance of caring for those who are poor.

(2) James is concerned with violence- especially with the violence people can do to each other with their words, and the violence the rich can do to the poor through dishonesty.

(3) The necessity of not only hearing God's teaching, but also doing it !

Faith must lead to action. Christians should not commit acts of violence on behalf of the poor-this is not the sort of action James supports. Instead, Christians should wait for God to bring justice into the world and while they are waiting, they should care for the poor around them.

Christology

This book is rich in its Christology. Christ is the object of our faith (2:1), the one in whose name and by whose power we perform our ministry (5:14, 15), the Rewarder of those who are steadfast in the midst of trials (1:12), and the coming one for whom we patiently wait (5:7-9). James identifies Christ as the glory (2:1), referring to the Shekinah, the glorious manifestation of the presence of God among His people. Not only glorious Himself, He is the divine glory, the presence of God on earth (Luke 2:30-32, John 1:14, Heb. 1:3). In the book, we can see the strong influence of the Lord in the life of James.

Pneumatology

The letter specifically mentions the Holy Spirit only in 4:5, which states the indwelling Spirit's strong desire for our undivided loyalty, jealously brooking no rivals.

Out Line

1. Salutation 1:1
2. Practical religion and trials 1:2-18
3. Practical religion and God's Word 1:19-27
4. Practical religion and speech 3:1-18
5. Practical religion and human relationship 2:1-26
6. Practical religion and worldliness 4:1-12
7. Practical religion and business affairs 4:13-5:6
8. Final appeals 5:7-20

Application

The book calls for ethical living based on the gospel. James gives a practical exposition of pure and undefiled religion (1:27). His two fundamental emphases are personal growth in spiritual life and sensitivity in social relationships. Any faith that does not deal with both personal and social issues is a dead faith. The message of James speaks especially to those who are inclined to take their way to heaven instead of walk their way there. So, we should always keep in mind that the good works are not the means to salvation but rather are the product of salvation. Though man is not justified by the law of works, he is justified by the law of faith-works.

PETRUINE LETTERS

I and II letters of Peter are known as the Petruine letters. These letters mainly describe about the persecution of the believers, as the cost of the true disciples of Jesus Christ, the Lord and Saviour of the universe.

I PETER

In the year A.D. 64, Emperor Nero decided to exterminate Christianity. Because of intense persecution, many of the believers left their homes in Jerusalem (1:6-7). Peter writes his letter to them to encourage them to stand true and endure the suffering for the sake of Christ and in His strength, no matter how intense it became. He seeks to change their focus from the difficulties at hand to the glory to come. The idea of suffering and hope saturate this letter.

Authorship and Date

The author of the document in the New Testament designated I Peter is identified as Peter, an apostle of Jesus (1:1). Traditionally and already in the ancient church, this apostle has been considered the author of I Peter. Tradition places the death of Peter in AD 64 during the Neronic persecutions. The content of 1st epistle, reflecting impending persecutions suggest a date shortly before the death of Peter. Peter appears to be in Rome while writing the letter.

Purpose

Peter's first readers were being persecuted and were suffering simply because they were Christians. Peter reminds them that their real hope is in the life to come. He encourages them to endure hardship and live godly lives in the meantime, awaiting the return of Christ.

Theme and Theology

The basic theme of I Peter is "the living hope in the midst of suffering." This paradox of rejoicing in suffering is a unique feature of Christianity. However, the example of Christ inspires the

Christians and provides a pattern to follow (2:21). This living hope in God (1:21) carries one through the fiery trials (4:12) and sufferings. The recipients of I Peter are experiencing persecutions and are faced with the prospect of similar sufferings. This is the privilege of the child of God – to be a partaker of Christ's sufferings (4:13). In the light of the living hope possessed by a Christian, he can rejoice in the midst of suffering (1:6,8, 4:13).

The theological significance of this epistle relates basically to the theme suggested above-living hope in the midst of suffering. Another significant theological motif in this epistle is the emphasis on the sovereignty of God. The redemptive work of Jesus was foreordained before the foundation of the world (1:2). The people of God are chosen and destined by God (2:9). These past demonstrations of God's sovereignty are the basis for the living hope, which looks with confidence to the future and its glory, which the Christians will share (5:1-10).

Christology

In 4 separate passages Peter links Christ's sacrificial sufferings with His glory that followed death (1:11; 3:18; 4:13; 5:1). The letter details the fruits of Christ's suffering and victory, including the provision for a new life now and hope for the future (1:3,18,19; 3:18). Anticipation of Christ's return in glory causes believers to rejoice (1:4-7).

Pneumatology

The Holy Spirit is active in the entire process of salvation: the Spirit of Christ testified beforehand concerning the cross and glory (1:11); Christ was raised from the death by the Spirit (3:18); Evangelist preached by the Spirit, believers responded in obedience through the Spirit (1:2,22).

Out Line

1.   Introduction 1:1-2
2.   Hard times and salvation 1:3-12
3.   A life of holiness 1:13-25
4.   God's chosen people 2:1-10

5.   A life of submission 2:11-3:12
6.   Hard times and glory 3:13-5:11
7.   Conclusion 5:12-14

Application

Since all true Christians experience hostility from an ungodly world, the call to patience and holiness amidst suffering is applicable to all. Persecution of Christians is as great in many areas of the world today, as it was in the first century and I Peter offers hope to those suffering for Christ's sake. Suffering purifies and proves the believer's faith and character.

II PETER

About 3 years after Peter wrote his 1st letter to the Christians in Asia Minor, he wrote again. Unlike his first letter, where he addressed how they should respond to suffering from without, this letter concerns itself almost exclusively with dangers from within the church.

Instead of facing trials brought on by the hostilities of other people on Christianity, the churches of Asia Minor were now facing serious attacks from those who seemed to be 'friendly' to the faith. False teachers were infiltrating the churches and turning many from the pure and sincere faith with which they had began. Peter also wants to inform his first readers how to handle those who have rejected the Lord and His truth.

Authorship and Date

The author identifies himself in the opening verse as 'Simon' Peter, a servant and apostle of Jesus Christ. We can surmise from the letter itself that Peter anticipates his own death shortly (1:14), which would give us a date of about A.D. 67. Peter was writing from the city of Rome.

Purpose

Following were the purposes of writing this letter:

(1)   To urge Christian growth.
(2)   To identify false teaching.

(3) To have an 'eye' towards Christ's return.

(4) Ultimately, the purpose of II Peter is to warn and instruct the churches to meet the new challenges that a later age would thrust upon them. It is an identifying personal letter to the church.

Theme and Theology

The one who claims to know God should guard himself against the teachings of false teachers and live their life with an 'eye' toward Christ's second coming.

This epistle covers creation, prophecy, law, judgment, cosmology[22] and atonement. It is of prime importance in the understanding of inspiration, revelation and inerrancy. The ethical application of the principle of the Parousia[23] is carried through out the book. Peter was not allegorizing the second coming, but he was demonstrating the important concern that each age has a response and a duty to perform, until Christ's coming.

Christology

The deity of Christ is evident in the way that God and Christ are closely linked in 1:1,2. God knows Christ as His Son (1:17). The divine purpose and activity are centered in Jesus Christ, as His grace and power are given to believers (1:2,3,8; 2:9) who are to look for His coming. (1:16).

Pneumatology

Holy Spirit's work is in moving the human authors of the prophetic scripture (1:20). However, the Spirit is obviously at work in providing the divine power that makes possible growth in the grace and knowledge of Christ (1:2-8; 3:18).

---

[22] It is the science of the origin and development of the universe.

[23] Parousia is an eschatological terminology which tells about the happenings or events of the future things. The Greek word for what we usually call in English is Christ's second coming (Matt. 10:23; II Pet. 1:16).

Out Line

1) Greeting 1:1-2
2) Try hard to grow 1:3-15
3) Our Lord's powerful return 1:16-21
4) Description of false teachers 2:1-22
5) Judgment day is approaching 3:1-10
6) New heaven and earth 3:11-16
7) Conclusion 3:17-18

Application

The concerns in 2 Peter are also concerns of the contemporary church as it counteracts worldliness and humanistic philosophy. There are still false teachers who deal in half-truths regarding the Christian faith and this letter provides a clear response to them.

JOHANNINE LETTERS

I, II and III letters of John are known as the Johannine letters in New Testament which are very much applicable throughout the ages.

I JOHN

I John is a kind of family book because it outlines as to who are genuinely the members of the family of God. Clearly, John written at a time when there are many opposing claims about what it means to be true believers (followers) of Jesus.

Authorship and Date

The apostle John is the author of this letter. By inference from the fact that John spent the last three year of his life in Ephesus; it is reasonable to assume that this was a circular letter that went to the churches in Asia Minor. It is probable that I John was written in Ephesus. Given the fact that I John was written after the book of John and that book was written later in John's life, it is likely that I John was written between A.D. 85-95.

Purpose

John wrote this letter to expose certain false teachers, who denied the truth that Jesus is the eternal Son of God, who became a human being. It is also to teach the marks of true believers: love for fellow believers, obedience to Christ's commandments and confession that Christ became a human being. Finally, it is to encourage holy living and a discerning of false teachers.

Theme

Christians can be assured of their salvation in Christ and enjoy fellowship with God and one another as a result.

Christology

John emphasizes both the deity and the humanity of Jesus, declaring that in Him, God fully entered into human life. Jesus is our advocate with the father (2:1). He is the Savior, sent by God to rescue us from sin (1:7; 3:5; 4:14). Only through Him can we have eternal life (5:11,12). John presents the second coming of Jesus as an incentive to remain firm in the faith (2:28) and he gives assurance that our complete transformation into Christ's likeness will occur on His return.

Pneumatology

Three-fold ministry of the Holy Spirit can be found in this letter:

1. He assures us our relationship to Christ (3:24).
2. He testifies to the reality of the incarnation of Christ (4:2, 5:6-8).
3. He leads true believers into a full realization of the truth concerning Jesus and opposes the heretic who deny that truth. (2:20, 4:4).

Out Line

1. Participants of the fellowship 1:1-4
2. Light of the fellowship 1:5-2:29
3. Love of the fellowship 3:1-4:2
4. Way to the fellowship 5:1-12
5. Certainty of the fellowship 5:13-21

Application

The positive note of Christian certainty is prominent in I John. Christian truth is beyond the realm of speculation, because it is moored to the historical event of Jesus Christ. In addition, Christians possess the anointing and witness of the Holy Spirit to assure them of the truth about God, Christ and their own spiritual standing.

Three tests prove the genuineness of Christianity. The test of belief (4:2), the test of obedience (2:3) and the test of love (4:20). John brings all three tests together in 5:1 where he indicates that profession of Christianity is false unless it is characterized by correct belief, godly obedience and brotherly love. If the believer abides in Christ, he will not live in sin.

II JOHN

In this letter, John merely calls himself 'the elder'. This could refer to his age or stature in the churches or both. John penned this to a Christian lady and her family from Ephesus. It was probably written between A.D. 85-95. This letter repeats the same warnings as in I John against false teachers who deny that Christ has come in the flesh; that person does not know God.

Purpose

This letter was written to encourage a Christian lady and her family to walk in the truth and to warn them against false teachers who deny that Christ came to earth as a human being.

Theme

Christians must love and live in God's truth, but have nothing to do with error.

Christology

John presents both the deity of Christ (v.3) and His humanity (v.7). Anyone who denies the fundamental truth concerning the divine human person of Christ does not have God (v.9). John views fellowship as distinctive feature of Christian life, but he leaves no doubt that biblical fellowship is impossible where the doctrine of the person and work of Christ is denied or compromised.

Pneumatology

Although the epistle doesn't specifically mention the Holy Spirit, His ministry is evident, particularly in bearing witness to the truth concerning the Person of the Christ. The Spirit enables a true believer to discern false teachings and to abide in the doctrine of Chirst, the Savior.

Out Line

1.   Loving is truth v. 1-3
2.   Walking is truth v.v 4-6
3.   Abiding is truth v.v. 7-11
4.   Good-bye v.v. 12-13

Application

John's message is timeless. The epistle reminds us to receive Jesus as **the** son of God **(the=suggests His uniqueness)**, not as a son of God **(a=suggests He is one among many sons of God)**. John warns about those who advance beyond the doctrine of Christ, accepting new teaching and leaving apostolic doctrine behind (v.9). To receive such people is to be identified with their evil (v.11) and to run the risk of losing faith (v.8).

III JOHN

The apostle John is the author of this small letter. This book was written in Ephesus to Gaius, a friend of John because it does not deal with the false teachings about Christ. It may have been written earlier than I John or II John, perhaps in the early A.D.80s. This book is all about hospitality. John commends Gaius for entertaining travelling believers and criticizes Diotrephes for his lack of hospitality and outright hostility to God's people. John also commends Demetrius for his good reputation.

Purpose

John's primary purpose for writing seems to be to praise Gaius for his love for the Christians and identify a problem element in the church, a man named Diotrephes. It is sovereign to see how openly and swiftly the early church took care of its own difficulties.

Theme

Being spiritually and bodily healthy means following the truth, helping others and doing well.

Christology

The apostle presents Jesus as the Truth in whom we should walk. Devotion to Him motivates genuine teachers in their itinerant service (v.7). The lives of Gaius and Demetrius exactly harmonized with the teaching of Christ and gave strong witness to the power of His love. On the other hand, the attitude of Diotrephes shows a marked contrast to the true life in which Christ is to be first in everything.

Pneumatology

Holy Spirit enables believers to walk in the truth and empowers itinerant missionaries in their ministries. The fruit of the Spirit is evident in the lives of Gaius and Demetrius.

Out Line

1. Following the way of truth v.v. 2-4
2. Helping the brethren v.v. 5-8
3. Rejecting evil and doing good v.v. 9-12

Application

The letter portrays the church as a family united by bonds of love, with its members extending gracious hospitality toward one another. However, selfish ambition and factious jealousy imperil the church's fellowship and its members must guard against such attitudes and strive to maintain a loving relationship with each other. Christianity is a practical walk in truth and love.

JUDE

This book is about the warnings about false teachers. Although the writer wanted to write to his audience about salvation, he felt it necessary to warn them about false teaching and false teachers that have come their way. The false teachers he has in mind are evil people, just the sort of people Jesus warned would be coming. The work of such people divides Christ's church and their presence is a reminder of the need for renewed faithfulness and truth in God.

Authorship and Date

The letter opens with a statement of identity and authorship, Jude, a servant of Jesus Christ, and a brother of James. It is interesting that Jude does not consider himself an apostle, but only a servant of the Lord (v.1, 17). It is difficult to ascertain from the letter itself just who the first readers were. Jude uses the of phrase 'dear friends' a numbers of times, possibly indicating that they are Palestinian Christians (Jews) because that was his homeland.

Purpose

He wrote to warn his first readers against false teachers and those who have turned against Jesus. He exhorted them to remain strong in faith and to fight actively against wrong teachings, not merely to avoid it. To Jude, the evil that was sweeping through the churches included immorality, rejection of the clear command of God, rejection of Jesus Christ as Savior and Lord, and an outright mockery of holy things. Jude challenges his first readers to defend the faith.

Theme and Theology

Christians need to be strong in the faith and active in fighting for truth. Diabolic dangers which comes from within and with out challenges us to pray. Truth and morality belong together. Certain judgment is going to fall upon these deviates and corruptors of the faith. Christians are to meet this situation with a faith that is built up or mature, with prayer in the Holy Spirit, with persistent reliance on the love of God, with a receptive and hopeful attitude toward the mercy of the Lord Jesus Christ and with solicitous evangelism which seeks to save some by pity and others by snatching them out of the fire even while hating the foul things they have made of themselves.

Christology

The present activity of the living Christ is assumed. Jude is His servant and He preserves His own (v.1), though false teachers deny Him (v.4). Believers await the future blessing of 'the mercy of our Lord Jesus Christ' unto eternal life (v.21).

Pneumatology

The Holy Spirit causes biblical teaching to come alive so that the Christian community is built up in its most holy faith (v. 20, 3, 4). This accomplishes through praying in the Holy Spirit.

Out Line

1. Greetings v.v. 1 - 2
2. Encouragement to fight for the faith v.v. 3 - 4
3. Worship and about evil people v.v. 5 - 16
4. Practical advice for standing strong v.v. 17 - 23
5. Praise v.v. 24-25

Application

Today, the godly commitment of Christians may be threatened but God's power is able to keep us from falling. Our responsibility is to build ourselves up in truth through praying in the Holy Spirit and to anticipate our final salvation. The scriptures are our resources. At the same time, we are to be alert and vocal in warning those who are being swayed by false, humanistic philosophies prevalent today.

PROPHECY

The book of Revelation is the kind of book in the New Testament which is known as prophecy. This book is the revelation of Jesus Christ.

REVELATION

The word translated 'revelation' simply means unveiling; it gives English word apocalypse, which, unfortunately, is today a synonymn for chaos and catastrophe. The verb simply means 'to uncover', 'to reveal', 'to make manifest'. In this book, the Holy Spirit pulls back the curtain and gives us the privilege of seeing the glorified Christ in heaven and the fulfillment of His sovereign purpose in the world.

In other words, Revelation is an open book in which God reveals His plans and purposes to His church. When Daniel finished writing his prophecy, he was instructed to shut the book and seal it (Dan. 12:4) but John was given opposite instructions; "seal not the saying of the prophecy of this book" (Rev. 22:10). Why ? Since Calvary, the resurrection and the coming of the Holy Spirit,God has ushered in the last days (Heb. 1: 1-2) and in fulfilling His hidden purposes in this world, the time is at hand (Rev. 1: 3; 22:10).

This book is the last book of the Holy Bible, which belongs to a class of biblical writing known as Apocalyptic. It is the only one of its kind is the New Testament. Apocalyptic writings in the Old Testament include Daniel, Ezekiel and Zechariah. This type of literature is normally characterized by:

(1) Extensive use of symbols and visions
(2) God's people are portrayed as suffering unjustly.
(3) It almost always has to do with future events.

Authorship and Date

The apostle John wrote Revelation, his last letter, while he was held prisoner on the island of Patmos, 35 miles off the coast of Asia Minor. Tradition tells us that John was exiled here under the reign of the Roman Emperor Domitian around A.D. 94.

There were three cycles of persecution during the 2nd half of the first century. Nero was the first, in the middle sixties. Domitians was the second between A.D. 84-96 and Trojans was the last, in the late nineties.

These were perilous and dangerous times for believers. They were crucified, burned alive, thrown to lions and forced to kill one another as gladiators. And signs of corruption were beginning to appear within the church as well. It is to this decaying and wicked age that John is called to write this letter of God's ultimate triumph.

This letter was written to the seven churches of Asia viz: Ephesus,[24] Smyrna,[25] Pergamum,[26] Thyatira,[27] Sardis,[28] Philadelphia,[29] and Laodicea.[30]

Purpose

The book of Revelation encourages Christians to stand firm amidst persecution; warns them against turning away from Jesus, and calls them to be faithful. The book gives a loud and clear warning to unbelievers about the judgment of God on sin, but it also contains severe exhortations to God's people to shape up.

Theme and Theology

Revelation shows who Jesus Christ is and what is His work in the present and future. Jesus is the head of the church, the judge and reward – giver of the future and the Eternal one who will welcome faithful believers into the new heavens and earth forever and ever.

The overriding theme of the book is the return of Jesus Christ to defeat all evil and to establish His reign. It is definitely a book of victory and His people are seen as overcomers (2:7, 11, 17, 26; 3:5, 12, 21; 11:7; 12:11). Through eyes of unbelief, Jesus Christ and His church are defeated in this world, but through eyes of faith,

---

[24] Apostolic church (33 – 200 A.D.). It is fully purposed church. Jerusalem was destroyed in A.D. 70; the persecutions really began in Roman Empire (I Pet 4:17). Diana worship in the city.

[25] Suffering church (200–350 A.D.). It is the suffering church or the persecuted church. Persecution continued untill Constantine about 310 A. D.

[26] Imperial church (350 –500). Christianity was made state religion of Rome about 400 A. D.. The city still exists and practice Emperor worship.

[27] Papal church (500 – 1000 A. D.). The church of compromise. It was also the suffering church.

[28] Dead church (1000 – 1500 A. D.). The crusades started. Much persecution also added.

[29] Brotherly Love (1500 – 1900 A. D.). It was the Reformation church. In 1870 A. D., the loss of temporal power by Papal church. Less persecutions. Many missionaries sent into world for Jesus. This period was the golden era of church history because she was given task of spreading the gospel.

[30] People pleasing church; Poor church (1900 - ??? A.D.). It is also the golden era of the church history because she is given the significant task of spreading the gospel.

He and His people are the true victors. The titles given to God in Revelation make it clear that He is certainly able to work out His divine purposes in human history. He is the Alpha and Omega: He is the beginning and the end. He is the eternal God. He is also the Almighty, able to do anything.

John 's revelation is primarily an appeal for resistance to all demands of the cult[31] of emperor worship. The glories and privileges of martyrdom are extolled throughout the book. The souls of those who have been slain are sheltered beneath the heavenly altar. A voice from heaven declares that all who will die as Christians are blessed (14:13). The author sees them standing by the glassy sea in heaven, singing a song of praise to God as did Moses and his followers (15:2-4). Their participation with the Lamb in the last war against paganism (19:14).[32] They reign with Him for a 1000 years as judges, priests and kings and they escape the second death (20:6).

---

[31] Oxford American Dictionary defines it as a system of religious worship especially as expressed in ritual ; a devotion to a person or thing. People join cults because they have spiritual, emotional or social needs that are not met.

If a religious group has one or more of the following characteristics, it may be a cult according to the chart entitled Christianity, Cults and Religions published by Rose Publishing House, USA:1) A leader who claims to be a divine. 2) Rejection of all other churches. 3) Control over member's activities and friendships. 4) A special diet. 5) Chants using religious phrases or words. 6) Sleep deprivation. 7) No privacy. 8) Overpowering demonstrations of love. 9) Control over finances, financial resources or financial decisions. 10) Leadership that does not tolerate the honest questions.

[32] It is the term used in several senses. It has been used to describe the religious and ethical system of the pre-Christian era, particularly those of classical culture. Secondly, in a second sense, the term paganism is used to describe the religious, moral and philosophical out look of those who have heard the Gospel and who have rejected the Biblical offer of salvation in favour of some other form of religious and philosophical system, e.g. materialism. This modern paganism is not a result of an ignorance of the gospel message, but rather of a deep- seated hatred for Christianity and it seems to interpret life in terms of non-Christian principles. In a third sense,it is described as the religious and moral state of those civilized and uncivilized peoples of the present day who have not yet been evangelized and who are living in the darkness of unbelief, superstition and idolatry and the hardness of their hearts.

Christology

Although Jesus' earthly ministry is telescoped between His incarnation and ascension in 12 : 5, Revelation asserts that the Son of God, as the Lamb, has completely finished His redemptive work (1:5, 6). By His blood, sinners have been forgiven, cleansed (5:6, 9, 7:14, 12:11), liberated (1:5) and made kings and priests (1:6, 5:10). All ensuring manifestations of His applied victory are based in His finished work on the cross, hence, Satan has been defeated (12: 7–12) and bound (20:1–3). Jesus rose from the dead, is enthroned as absolute sovereign over all creation (1:5, 2:27). He is the King of Kings and Lord of Lords (17:14, 19:16) and is entitled to the same ascriptions of adoration as God, the Creator (5:12-14). As the one who has conquered, He has the rightful authority and the power to control all the forces of evil and their consequences for His purposes of judgment and salvation (6:1-7:17). The Lamb is on the throne (4:1-5:14, 22:3).

The Lamb is the God who is coming (1:7, 8, 11:17) to consummate His eternal plan, to complete the creation of the new community of His people in a new heaven and a new earth (21:1) and to restore the blessings of the paradise of God (22:2-5). The Lamb is the goal of all history (22:13).

Pneumatology

In this book, the description of the Holy Spirit is as the Seven Spirits of God (1:4, 3:1). Seven is the number of perfection. Thus, Holy Spirit is denoted in terms of the perfection of His dynamic, manifold activity. The Seven Lamps of fire (4:5) suggest His illuminating, purifying and energizing ministries. The Spirit is the Spirit of prophecy. Every genuine prophecy is inspired by the Holy Spirit and bears witness to Jesus (19:10). The Spirit is working continuously in and through the church to invite those who remain outside the city of God to enter. The Spirit penetrates the present experience of those who hear with foretastes of the Kingdom's future fulfillment.

Distinctive Characterstics

1.   It is a Christ-centred book

It magnifies the greatness and glory of Jesus Christ. The book is after all, the revelation of Jesus Christ and not simply the revelation of future events.

2.   It is an open book

John was told not to seal the book (22:10) because it contained message for God's people.

3.   It is a book filled with symbols

Biblical symbols are timeless in their message and timeless in their content. The book of Revelation is full of symbols like beast, horse etc.

4.   It is a book of prophecy

Almost all chapters except the letter to 7 churches, deals with the prophetic revelation.

5.   It is a majestic book

Revelation is the book of the throne for the word 'throne' is found 46 times throughout this book. This book magnifies the sovereignty of God. Christ is presented in His glory and dominion.

6.   It is a climatic book

Revelation is the climax of the Bible. All that began in Genesis will be completed and fulfilled in keeping with God's sovereign will. He is the Alpha and Omega, the beginning and the end (1:8). What God starts, He finishes.

Out Line

1.   Introduction 1:1-8
2.   Jesus among the seven churches 1:9-20
3.   The letters to the seven churches ch. 2-3
4.   The throne, the scroll and the Lamb ch. 4-5
5.   The seven seals 6:1-8:1
6.   The seven trumpets 8:2-11:19

7. Various personages and events chs 12-14
8. The seven bowls chs 15-16
9. Babylon : The great prostitute 17:1-19:5
10. Praise for the wedding of the lamb 19:6-10
11. The return of Christ 19:11-21
12. The thousand years 20:1-6
13. Satan's doom 20:7-10
14. Great white throne judgment 20:11-15
15. New heaven, new earth, new Jerusalem 21:1-22:5
16. Conclusion 22:6-21

Application

God has created the orders of community i.e., marriage and the family economic activity, government and the state (Rom. 13:1-7, I Tim. 2: 1,2). Satan, unable to create anything, tempts others to distort and misuse what God has created. Christians must pray, courageously endure, and patiently accept the consequences of obeying the God whose image and seal they bear (Mark 12:16,17, Acts 4:19).

Behind the appearances of the pomp and power of the world, there is the reality of the absolute sovereignty of the Lord God who is the Lamb, which ensures the ultimate doom of sin and evil. God is utilizing all the forces of evil, all the consequences of sin, even the suffering of his saints, to accomplish His own purposes. Believers undergoing persecution need to know that their sufferings are not meaningless, and ultimately they will be vindicated. The main spring of Christian hope and courage is the certainty that the enemy has been defeated and is doomed and that followers of the Lamb are not fighting a losing cause. He has already overcome, and therefore they can and will be over comers. Those who overcome the world, the flesh and the devil will receive the everlasting rewards.

BIBLIOGRAPHY

Bullock, Harsell C. *An Introduction to the Old Testament Prophetic Books*. Chicago: Moody Press, 1986.

Buttrick, George Arthur (ed.). *The Interpreter's Dictionary of the Bible*, vol.3. Nashville: Abingdon Press, 1962.

Mickelsen, Alvera and Berkeley (eds.). *The Picture Bible Dictionary*. England: Chariot Books, 1993.

MacArthur, John (ed.). *The MacArthur Study Bible*. London: Word Publishing, 1997.

Barker, Kenneth (ed.). *The NIV Study Bible*. Michigan: Zondervan Bible Publishers, 1985.

Lindsell, Harold (ed). *The People's Study Bible*. Wheaton: Tyndale House Publishers, 1986.

Life Application Study Bible: The Living Bible. Wheaton: Tyndale House Publishers, 1988.

Unger, Messill F. (ed). *The New Unger's Bible Dictionary*. Chicago: Moody Press, 1988.

Harrison, Everelt F. (ed). *Baker's Dictionary of Theology*. Michigan: Baker Book House, 1979.

Unger, Merrill F. *The Hodder Bible Handbook* : London: Hodder and Stoughton, 1984.

Hayford, Jack W. (ed). *Spirit Filled Life Bible*. London: Thomas Nelson Publishers, 1991.

Green, Joel B. and Tramper Longman (eds). *The Everyday Study Bible*. London: Word Publishing, 1996.

Barker, Kenneth L. and J. R. Kohlenberger (eds). *Zondervan NIV Bible Commentary*, Vol.1. Michigan: Zondervan Publishing House, 1994.

Honeycatt Roy. *Layman's Bible Book Commentary*, Vol. 3. Tennessee: Boardman Press, 1979.

Kent, Dan G. *Layman's Bible Book Commentary*, Vol. 4. Tennessee: Boardman Press, 1980.

Wiseman, D.J. (ed) *Tyndale Old Testament Commentary: Judges and Ruth*. England: Inter-varsity Press, 1968.

Tenney, Merrill C. *The Zondervan Pictorial Encyclopedia of the Bible*,Vol.5. Michigan: Zondervan Publishing House, 1977.

Traylor, John H. *Layman's Bible Book Commentary*, Vol. 6. Tennessee: Boardman Press, 1981.

Andersen, Francis I. *Tyndale Old Testament Commentaries : Job*. England: Inter-Varsity Press.

Layman, Charles M.(ed). *Wisdom Literature and Poetry*. Nashville: Abingdon Press, 1984.

Hwang, Andrew and Samuel, Gath. *Song Of Songs* in Asia Bible Commentary edited by Bruce Nicolas. Bangalore : Theological Book Trust, 2001.

Zuck, Roy B.(ed) *A Biblical Theology of the Old Testament*. Chicago : Moody Press, 1991.

Vos, Howard F. *Effective Bible Study*. Michigan: Lamplighter Books, 1965.

Mears, Henrietta C *What the Bible is All About*. Minnesota: The Billy Graham E.Association, 1966.

Phillips, John. *Exploring the Scriptures*. Chicago : Moody Press, 1968.

Barr, James. *Holy Scripture*. Philadelphia: The Westminster Press, 1983.

MacDonald, L. Martin. *The Formation of the Christian Biblical Canon*. Nashville: Abingdon Press, 1988.

Schwarz, John. *Christian Faith*. Minnesota : Bethany House Publishers, 1999.

Dyrness, William. *Themes in Old Testament Theology*. Illinois : Inter-varsity Press, 1979.

Boadt, Lawrence. *Reading the Old Testament*. New York: Paulist Press, 1984.

Merrill, Eugene H. *An Historical Survey of the Old Testament*. Michigan: Baker Book House, 1991.

Barton, John. *Reading the Old Testament*. Philadelphia: The Westminster Press, 1984.

Foreman, Kenneth J. and Others. *The Layman's Bible Commentary*: Introduction to the Bible. Richmond: John Knox Press, 1965.

Smith, William. *A Dictionary of The Bible*. Michigan: Zondervan Publishing House, 1967.

Miller, Madeleine S. and Lane J. *Harper's Bible Dictionary*. London : Harper and Row, Publishers, 1961.

Mead, Frank S. *The Encyclopedia of Religious Quotations*. New Jersey : Fleming H. Revell Company, 1965.

Wilmington, H.L. *Wilmington's Book Of Bible Lists*. Wheaton: Tyndale House Publishers, 1987.

Hinson, David F. *The Books of the Old Testament*. New Delhi: ISPCK, 1993.

Unger, Merrill F. and Larson G.N. *The Hodder Bible Handbook*. London: Hodder and Stonghton, 1984.

Barclay, William. *The Gospel of Matthew*. Philadelphia : The Westminster Press, 1975.

France, R.T. *Tyndale New Testament Commentaries : Matthew*. England: Inter- varsity Press, 1985.

Gaebelein, Frank E. (ed). *The Expositors Bible Commentary*, Vol.8. Michigan: Regency Reference Library, 1984.

Ironside, H.A. *Expository Notes on the Gospel of Mark*. Bombay: Gospel Literature Service, 1983.

Peterson, Hugh R. *A Study of the Gospel of Mark*. Tennessee: Convention Press, 1958.

Stagg, Frank. *Studies in Luke's Gospel*. Tennessee: Convention Press, 1967.

Geldenhuys, Norval. *The Gospel of Luke*. Michigan: W.M.B.E. Publishing Company, 1988.

Tresch, John W. and Griffin K. *Book Alive*. Tennessee: Convention. Press, 1973.

Ironside, H.A. *Romans*. Texas: Carroll Thompson Ministry, 1978.

Thompson, Carroll. *Romans*. Texas: Carroll Thompson Ministry, 1978.

Brown, Roger. *A Guide to Romans*. New Delhi: ISPCK, 1995.

Mare, W. Harold. *1 Corinthians*. The Expositors Bible Commentary, Vol.10. Michigan: Regency Reference Library, 1976

MacGorman, J. W. *L. B. B. Commentary, Vol. 20*. Tennessee: Broadman Press, 1980.

MacArthur, John. *The MacArthur N.T. Commentaries: Galatians*. Pune: Grace to India, 1997.

Tenney, Merrill C. (ed). *The Zondervan Pictorial Encyclopedia of the Bible*, Vol. 2. Michigan : Zondervan Publishing House, 1977.

Jenson, Irving L. *Jensens' Survey of the New Testament*. Chicago: Moody Press, 1981.

The Teachers Outline and Study Bible: *Galatians*. U.S.A : Alpha and Omega Ministries, Inc, 1994.

The Teachers Outline and Study Bible: *Ephesians*. U.S.A: Alpha and Omega Ministries, Inc, 1994.

The Teachers Outline and Study Bible: *Colossians*. U.S.A: Alpha and Omega Ministries, Inc, 1994.

Wiersbe, Warren W. *Be Rich: Ephesians* Bombay : Gospel Literature Service, 1991.

Stott, John. *Essential Fellowship: The Message of Ephesians*. Leicester: Inter-varsity Press, 1989.

Hawthorne, Gerald F and others(eds). *Dictionary of Paul and His Letter*. England : Inter-varsity Press, 1993.

Gould, Dana (ed). *Shepherd's Notes: Philippians, Colossians, Philemon*. Tennessee: Boardman and Holman Publishers, 1997.

Barclay, William. *The Letters to the Philippians, Colossians and Thessalonians*: Philadelphia : The Westminster Press,1975.

Hargreaves, John. *A Guide to Philippians*. New Delhi: ISPCK,1994.

Motyer, Alec. *The Message of Philippians*. England: Inter-varsity Press, 1984.

Wiersbe, Warren. *Be Victorious: Revelation*. England: Victor Books, 1985.

Laymon, Charles M.(ed). *Interpreters Concise Commentary: Revelation and the General Epistles.* Nashville: Abingdon Press, 1983.

Enns, Paul P. *Shepherd's Notes: Ezekiel.* Tennessee: Boardman and Holman Publishers, 1998.

Kennedy, John. *Prophecy for Today.* Bombay : Gospel Literature Service, 1993.

McGee, J. Vernon. *Amos and Obadiah.* California: Thru' the Bible Books, 1978.

Jensen, Irving L. *Minor Prophets of Israel.* Chicago: The Moody Press, 1975.

Johnson, L.D. *An Introduction to the Bible.* Tennessee: Convention Press, 1969.

Barclay, William. *Introducing the Bible.* Nashville: Abingdon Press, 1972.

Stott, John. *Understanding the Bible.* London: Scripture Union, 1988.

Dodd, C.H. *The Bible Today.* Britain: Cambridge University Press, 1956.

Grudem, Wayne. *Systematic Theology.* England: Inter-varsity Press, 1944.

Thomas, Kurian. *Dharmavigyan Pranali.* Itarsi: Central India Theological Seminary, 1999.

Jenson, Irving L. *Simply Understanding the Bible.* Minneapolis: World Wide Publications,1990.

Cho, Joon Sang. *An Introduction to Bible's 66 Books.* Bangalore: Joon Sang Cho, 2004.

Motyer, Stephen. *Men with a Message.* England: Evangelical Literature Trust, 1994.

Basic Information about the Bible. USA: Christian Literature and Bible Centre Inc.

Bible Dictionary and Concordance. Tennessee: Boardman and Holman Publishers, 1998

Enns, Paul. *The Moody Handbook of Theology.* Chicago: Moody Press, 1989.

Kelly, Balmer H. *The Layman's Bible Commentary, Vol. 1.* Richmond: John Knox Press, 1965.

Hinson, David F. *The Books of the Old Testament.* Delhi: ISPCK, 1992.

Stewart, Don. *What Everyone Needs to Know about Jesus.* California: Dart Press.

Buttrick, George Arthur (ed.). *The Interpreter's Bible Commentary,* Vol. 1. Tennessee: Abingdon Press, 1980.

The Word in Life Study Bible. London: Thomas Nelson Publishers, 1996.

Alexander, David and Pat (eds.). *Eerdmans' Handbook to the Bible.* Michigan: W. B. E. Publishing Company, 1980.

Benware, Paul N. *Survey of the Old Testament.* Chicago: Moody Press, 1988.

Ro, Bong Rin and R. Eshenaur (eds.). *The Bible and Theology In Asian Context.* Bangalore: A.T.A, 1984.

www.ingramcontent.com/pod-product-compliance
Lightning Source LLC
Chambersburg PA
CBHW030547030726
47495CB00004B/1166